I0766351

# HER MONSTER

Everly Rose

Sitta Jayne

Immortal Mark Saga

Book 1

**Her Monster**
Immortal Mark Saga
Copyright © *Everly Rose, Sitta Jayne* 2025
All Rights Reserved
This book is subject to the condition that no part of this book is to be reproduced, transmitted in any form or means; electronic or mechanical, stored in a retrieval system, photocopied, recorded, scanned, or otherwise. Any of these actions require the proper written permission of the author.

# Contents

## Insight

Thoughts of Him-

Eye contact is a dangerous, dangerous thing. Because now I see him everywhere. The intimacy of them lingering with my thoughts. That depth of raw emotion stirred a craving so deep. He fucked me over with a stare. Now my scribbles in the margins are all about him.

And they will forever be.

### Sadie

---

Thoughts of Her-

A simple glance turned into an obsession. She was the one who broke down the walls surrounding his icy heart. Her hands caressed it slowly, making it beat once more. His mating mark shone like a beacon on her skin. She became his world.

She was his everything.

### Damien

---

# Author Humor

*Sitta-* So you think they are ready for this book? You know, Damien can be a little much sometimes.

*Everly-* What? No way. He is one of my favorite characters along with Sadie.

*Sitta-* So you like those men who are large in charge?

*Everly-* NODS HER HEAD- You damn well know it.

*Sitta-* And you like how I write the males, do ya?

*Everly- CRACKS A SMILE-* You know I do. They are swoon-worthy.

*Sitta- laughs-* Got to make my girls happy. So, what adventure should we start next?

*Everly-* Let's tell the hellhound's story.

*Sitta-* The Scottish hound. He is definitely swoon-worthy and a handful.

# Acknowledgement

We both want to say thank you to everyone for their support in our writing journey. This is a dream come true for both of us. Creating worlds and bringing them to life. We so very much appreciate you taking a chance on an unknown story and allowing these characters into your imagination.

To our families that endure us living simultaneously in two different worlds-the real one and the one within these pages. Thank you for believing.

Why do writer's write? Because they must. And a hope that their words can reach across time and space and touch another human heart.

# Prologue

In the rugged terrain of Sicily, where the sun cast long shadows over the jagged peaks and the air crackled with untold tales, a man meticulously pieced together his empire from the shards of his shattered heart.

Damien, the leader of the Sicilian mafia, reigned at the apex of authority—a throne constructed upon a foundation of fear and treachery.

To the outside world, he was a fearsome deity, revered by some and despised by others. Yet beneath the steely exterior lay a heart encased in layers of grief and fury.

The passage of years had done little to relieve the agony of the fateful day when his world collapsed, when love morphed into a weapon that seared his very essence.

The echoes of his wife's betrayal rang through the silence of his home, and the absence of his son left a wound that stubbornly refused to close.

Swearing to never lower his defenses again, he embraced the enveloping darkness. Trust became an extravagance, and vulnerability a faded recollection.

But then she materialized—a woman whose slightest caress threatened to dismantle the fortressed walls he had erected. Possessing eyes reminiscent of pools of molten caramel and a spirit that danced with vitality, Sadie embodied everything he had renounced.

Her presence was both a boon and a bane, a delicate strand poised to weave its way through his barriers.

Might she unearth the tenderness buried beneath his scars, or would he yield to the impulse to repel her, safeguarding the remnants of his fractured soul?

As the tides of destiny began to shift, Damien found himself teetering on the edge of a decision—one that could either shatter him irrevocably or kindle an ember of hope he had long believed extinguished.

In a world where love resembled a battlefield, he was a warrior weary from the strife. Yet maybe, she could impart the lesson that even the most indomitable of fighters could rediscover love.

# Chapter 1

Damien realized the guys were concerned about him, but it didn't give them a reason to walk down memory lane. They had all been there and knew what the fuck had happened. Bane, Levi, and Enzo, all were slinging back beers and feeling all emotional, he guessed, but that didn't give these fuckers any reason to bring up his past or worry about his future. He loved these guys like brothers, and he would gladly take a bullet for them, without hesitation.

He knew they meant well, but Damien wouldn't get emotionally involved with a woman ever again, just sedating his need to fuck and nothing more. He was a complete and utter asshole, but he let every woman know that's all they would ever get with him; the best night of their fucking life. He aimed to please, and he didn't disappoint.

Enzo slid a beer down the bar to him. "Dame, it's been over two hundred years. You gotta let that shit go, or it will eat you alive. You deserve to be happy. Let it go, man."

Damien's hands clenched into fists, his knuckles cracking like gunshots. The air around him turned ice-cold as darkness bled from his skin like smoke. His shadows writhed along the walls, reaching toward Enzo with grasping fingers. When he looked up, his eyes had gone completely black—no iris, no white, just endless void.

Levi smacked Enzo across his chest. "What the fuck did you do that for?"

Damien picked up his beer and threw it towards Enzo's head. He ducked out of the way, and it slammed against the back wall.

"Enzo, you fucking asshole. You know how much I loved my wife. I gave her everything, my heart, soul, what remained of my kingdom and my baby. I gave her the world, and she betrayed me!! She was sleeping with the enemy and feeding me nothing but lies. All she wanted was my wealth and status, nothing more. She killed my son. My sweet baby boy. That fucking bitch took the most precious gift away from me. The one thing I loved more than anything. So I fucking ended her miserable life, and I promised myself that I would never trust another again. Do you know what happens when you lose a child? You fucking die inside!"

Levi was the quiet one of them all, and tears spilled from his eyes. His wife had just given birth to their son a month ago, and Damien couldn't bring himself to visit Levi because all he would see was his baby boy's face. It still haunts him to this day.

"I fucking failed him, and I made a vow to Ryder that I would always protect him, and I couldn't do it."

Levi put his arm around Damien's shoulder. "No parent should ever feel the pain of losing their child. I am sorry about that. But there are good women out there, and you deserve to be loved. Let that hate go, man. Not for anyone but yourself.

See, the thing is, the only person it is hurting is you. You are letting Sofia win. Don't let her win, Damien."

Levi might be right, but Damien couldn't let it go because it was too fucking raw still. How could he let it go when it cut so deep? Bone deep, and he wasn't sure if he could let another woman into his life.

Damien had given all of himself to her. He'd held nothing back just to get his heart ripped out. To do that again would turn him into the monster that no one would ever be prepared for.

He tried his best not to let his mind drift to the past, to the very moment his world came crashing to a halt. The moment he lost everything, the darkness grew within his heart. It was the day he refused to love another.

*Damien paced, holding his phone pressed to his ear. Listening to his friend Bane's voice crackle through the line and drone on and on about business deals that were insignificant in the grand scheme of his life was boring the hell out of him.*

*Glancing toward the bathroom, he could hear the soft splashes of water and the gentle coos of his three-month-old son, Ryder, as Sofia bathed him. A fleeting smile crossed his lips; moments like this made the weight of his responsibilities feel lighter.*

*But then, the laughter turned to silence, and an eerie stillness enveloped the house. Before he could register the change, a piercing scream shattered the calm, cutting through his thoughts like a knife. It was Sofia's voice, raw and desperate.*

***"Ryder!"***

*Damien's heart hit his feet. The phone slipped from his numb fingers, clattering against the hardwood as he bolted down the hall. His bare feet pounded the floor, each thundering step echoing Sofia's scream in his head. He slammed into the bathroom door frame, his shoulder cracking against the wood. The sight that greeted him sucked the air from his lungs—his worst fucking nightmare come to life.*

*Sofia knelt on the tiled floor, cradling their son in her arms. Ryder's tiny body lay motionless, his skin an unnatural shade of blue, and her sobs filled the air with a haunting melody of despair. Time slowed as Damien's world collapsed around him.*

*"Give him to me!" he shouted, desperation clawing at his throat.*

*He ripped Ryder from Sofia's trembling arms, instinct taking over. Kneeling beside his son, he fought to remember the techniques he'd once learned. He pressed down on Ryder's tiny chest, counting, praying, pleading for a miracle. But the seconds stretched into an eternity, and no breath came, no sign of life flickered in those delicate features.*

*His hands stilled on Ryder's chest. The silence stretched, broken only by Sofia's ragged breathing. Damien pressed his ear to his son's lips, desperate for even the whisper of breath. Nothing. The tiny chest under his palms remained motionless. A sound tore from his throat—raw, animalistic, barely human. He looked up, the weight of his grief crashing down like a tidal wave. Sofia stood before him, her face a mask of anguish and something darker. Her eyes, once filled with love, now burned with a cold, unyielding truth.*

*"I never loved you, Damien," she spat, her voice shaking with emotion. "I just took the only thing you truly loved away from you."*

*The words slammed into him like a physical blow, stealing his breath. His vision blurred as the room tilted sideways. Sofia's face wavered above him, her mouth still moving, but all he could hear was the roar of blood in his ears. His son's lifeless body grew heavy in his arms, and something deep inside his chest cracked—not his ribs, but something far more vital. In that moment, he felt the walls of his heart rise, brick by brick, determined never to let anyone in again.*

*As he cradled his son's lifeless body, an icy void replaced the warmth of love, and the God of Monsters made a vow to never love again...*

Sweat covered Damien as a hand clasped his shoulder, pulling him out of his recurring nightmare and back to reality, with a Scottish hellhound staring him in the face.

"Boss, are ye alright? Ye're drenched in sweat. I told the lads never to mention Sofia again. I know how hard that is for ye— a constant reminder of losin' your boy."

Damien picked up the glass of whiskey and slung it back in one gulp. "I miss my boy."

Bane felt his heart clench; he could never imagine losin' a child. "I wish I could bring him back. Ye drink until ye canna feel any pain. I'll make sure ye get home safe."

# Chapter 2

**The more control you have over yourself, the less others have over you—**

And that was Sadie's problem. Her stomach had been eating itself for three days straight when Donovan Caine crossed her path. The kind of desperation that made you consider things your mother would have slapped you for thinking. She didn't realize she was getting in bed with the devil. Not a literal bed because she'd never slept with him and never would. Her eyes opened rather quickly to the drug lord's world. But by then, she had a roof over her head, new clothes, a car, and cash in her pocket. And all that because she might have, by goof and golly, saved his life.

Right place, right time, or maybe wrong place, wrong time, she didn't know. But once he saw what she could do with a simple touch, even though she didn't have the ability to control it, he made sure she was in his debt. And she'd let it happen.

"I need you now." Donovan's text staring at her from her screen.

She didn't want to go. Her hands went cold just thinking about it. That look he'd get, like she was some kind of carnival trick he'd paid admission to see. Touch this, feel that, tell me what you see. Over and over until her head felt like it might split. The memory of last time sat heavy behind her eyes—that bone-deep weariness that came from having someone rifle through your soul like they were looking for loose change. Yet she had no one to call or turn to. She'd made her bed; she just needed to keep her sanity and bide her time.

For the most part, he was decent and fair, even if that word didn't exist in his vocabulary. She'd secretly hoped it was maybe, even slightly on a small scale, that she frightened him.

Sadie knew he was a bad guy. Correction—everyone did if you lived in Cali. Whispers followed his name from Seattle to San Diego. She'd heard truckers mention him at gas stations, seen bartenders go pale when someone brought up "that Caine guy." He was **The Guy** you did not want to cross; the word "mafia" was one she never let pass her lips because then this would all become too real. And in a reality like that, there could be no escape.

Yet their paths had crisscrossed one early autumn morning on the back streets of Santa Monica. That voice in the back of her head was shouting at her to walk away. But she'd stuffed it down deep, the way you swallow medicine that tastes like hell. That voice was smart. That voice knew the truth. And she'd shushed it.

She huddled back against a brick wall, the chill a real, painful dampness seeping through the thinness of her bargain basement jacket. The inky shadows growing on the walls of the building opposite, where she'd burrowed against a row of piled boxes stacked up against a bin.

Discarded newspapers and trash were thrown about by the wind as it funneled through the alley, lifting and pulling them to the mouth of the back lane where a bloom of voices grew louder but then faded away.

This was all Sadie's fault. She'd arrived at the shelter later than normal, and they were all full. If Maya had been working, she could maybe have snuck her in, but she wasn't. She'd even tried the alley behind the women's shelter, at least to be close by for the morning's meal, but it was closed off for sewer repairs.

From where she sat, she glanced toward the street beyond the pocket of shadows that were slowly lifting at the start of another day. The few early morning risers all going somewhere, all having a purpose, all having lives. She should move, make her way back to the shelter, and hopefully get some coffee and a danish.

Her hood was yanked off her head by a brutal pair of hands, her little corner of warmth in a random alley disturbed by two goons. And that's what they were.

Sadie knew street life; she lived it, on again, off again, for the last couple of years, depending on her money situation. This was typically a quiet row where no one usually bothered anyone. But not this morning.

"If you don't want to see your face marked up, you'll do what I ask. A black sedan will be pulling in here in the next fifteen minutes. Give him this bag. That's all. We'll be watching. If you don't?" The look on his face, and she knew it didn't have to be made clearer. "There's a hundred-dollar bill in it for you if you do." His hand lifted from his pocket with the bill there for her to see.

Sadie's first thought was that she could get a cheap room with that. Have a hot shower, a warm bed, and regroup. She knew this might be all kinds of stupid, and it probably was, but she nodded that she was on board, and they left the bag at her feet.

Minutes ticked by, and the purr of an engine as it came around the corner, the dark sedan coming to a stop not far from the bin she was using as a wind block. Her gaze dipped to the backpack, knowing that whatever was in it was not on the up and up. But her better judgment took a nose dive because she hadn't been able to afford even the cheapest room over the last few weeks.

Pushing herself up, her hand grasping the handle, she was a few steps in when the horror of emotion crept up through her arm and set her heart to racing.

*Visions of gunshots and blood sent her into a panic attack.* Her feet faltered as the back door opened, and there he stood. Her savior, the devil, one and the same. Her words mumbled, mostly incoherent, but he'd managed to understand.

"Don't open it... trap." Then the seizure hit, and she'd blacked out, her eyes opening a short time later to find herself in the back seat of the sedan, him staring at her.

"How did you know, ma petite?" His accent was slight, and she couldn't make out from where, but it was there.

Sadie's tongue was dry and stuck to the roof of her mouth. "I sometimes have visions. It's very random and not always right."

Her gaze was uneasy and unable to hold his. Because she was lying, and he knew she was lying.

"Fortunately for me, then, today you were correct. My name is Donovan, Donovan Caine, and you've earned yourself breakfast. So sit back, and after we eat, you and I can have a little talk."

He made it sound like she had an option when she didn't. He nodded to the two men in the front seats to continue, her gaze realizing that they weren't even in the same neighborhood anymore. What had happened that she'd missed?

Looking around for the bag but not seeing it.

"All will be explained. You're not in danger." Four words that she knew she should heed but didn't.

Because Sadie needed what he could give her to get what she wanted. Dominoes do happen, and you can't stop them. You can try, but all you catch is air trying to snatch them up.

How do you get out of a mess of your own making?

Slowly and very carefully. The underbelly of the mafia world was branded on family and loyalty. She wasn't family, but she'd stumbled her way in under the fallacy of the latter.

But building her life from the eggshells of her youth on the back of drug money? She knew she was screwed. She just didn't realize how badly or how her world was going to be flipped upside down.

She often wondered why a bird would stay inside their cage even when the door was left open. Now she knows why. Because there was a trap waiting.

# Chapter 3

Damien's phone buzzed at 5:47 AM. He glanced at the screen—Bane's name flashing—and slid to answer. "Do I want to know why you're calling me this fucking early, Hellhound? I haven't even made my first round yet, not to mention my first cup of coffee. This better be good news because I'm not in the mood for any shit."

Bane growled loudly on the other end. "Would ye get laid already! How long's it been, anyway?"

Damien clenched his jaw. "If you don't get to the fucking point, I'll send you to see my father, and you won't see your beautiful wife for days."

The threat of Tartarus—the deepest, darkest part of the underworld where the wicked were punished for their crimes— always made Bane squirm. His father was one of the first beings to exist, the primordial god of the underworld. It was said to be so deep that it would take nine days and nights for an anvil to fall from Earth and reach it. His mother, Gaia, wielded the power to create and destroy as the personification of Earth itself.

Damien held back laughter, knowing the old hellhound hated it when he threatened him with his parents. Bane had been by his side since day one, but sometimes it felt good to push his fucking buttons.

"Ye're such an arsehole, Damien. We've got a problem on our hands. Drake an' his lads are in town, causin' bother in the club. How do ye want tae handle it? There are humans here. I'll do my best tae get them out before the shite storm hits."

Drake. Damien's fingers tightened around the phone. Most vampires thought themselves entitled to everything, believing everyone was beneath them. Drake was the worst of them.

"I'll be there in ten minutes."

Damien pulled up to the front of his club, where a line of motorcycles stood to his left. He slammed the door to his Bugatti and strode into Enigma. Inside, Drake and his minions were acting like heathens, hollering and trying their best to grope the ladies. The scent of spilled whiskey and fear hung in the air. Normally, Damien would let his boys handle situations like this, but his mood had been shit for days, and they were about to get a firsthand lesson in who he truly was.

He sent out a wash of his powers, and no humans remained inside. Bane had gotten them out. His gaze locked on Drake, who had just grabbed Carmella's arm, jerking her onto his lap and leering as he told her how he was going to use her.

Hellfire ignited in Bane's eyes, and Damien winked his way as he stepped forward. Carmella looked up at her boss, a knowing smile on her lips. She knew shit was about to go down.

Damien held out his hand for Carmella to take. Drake sneered. "Who the fuck do you think you are?"

"My name is Damien Nikolas Messina, Leader of Della Mafia Sicilian." His voice dropped to barely above a whisper. "Enigma is my club, and Carmella works for me. Now be a good fucking boy and let her go."

Drake laughed, running a finger down Carmella's cheek. "Like I give a shit who you are. I'm just trying to show her a good time. If you choose not to let us be, then you'll have to deal with my Coven. They'll enjoy killing you."

Bane chuckled. "Ye just fucked up, Vamp."

Damien leaned closer to Drake, their noses almost touching. The temperature in the room dropped ten degrees. "Then let me introduce you to the monster I am. The God of Monsters, as a matter of fact. My father named me Typhon. Maybe you've heard of me, or maybe not. Either way, you are going to get a front row seat to who I really am."

Power coursed through him, awakening his hidden self. Immortal blood pumped through his veins. Superhuman strength and stamina flowed within him—a legacy of his lineage that made him resistant to injuries even from the Olympian gods. Typhon commanded the chaotic forces of hurricanes and tornadoes, and his monstrous form was a sight to behold.

As Drake released Carmella, terror washed over his pale features. In a moment of panic, he attempted to flash out of the club, only to find himself frozen by Damien's growing aura. The air crackled with energy as Damien transformed into his true form.

His torso remained that of a man, but his legs twisted into coils of vipers, hissing and ready to strike. His skull sprouted endless snake heads, each emitting the sounds of various creatures, while his glowing scarlet eyes instilled fear in anyone who dared to meet his gaze.

The club's atmosphere shifted from festive to frozen as the remaining patrons pressed themselves against the walls, realizing the danger that loomed.

Damien's jaw exhaled smoke like a furnace, and endless wings sprouted from his back, stirring the air around him and creating a tempest that rattled the very foundation of the club.

"Let me show you what happens when you disrespect me," Damien growled, his voice a chorus of hisses and roars.

Drake's bravado shattered; he stumbled backwards, his eyes wide with horror. "No! This can't be happening!"

With a swift motion, Damien unleashed his powers, enveloping Drake and his coven in a contained whirlwind of chaos. Shadows danced, and with a flick of his wrist, he summoned the fury of the storm. The ground trembled as torrents of wind and fire erupted around them, consuming the vampires in an inferno of rage.

As the flames slowly subsided, silence fell over the club. The remnants of Drake and his followers lay smoldering—a stark reminder of the consequences of their actions. Damien shifted back to his human form, the tension in his muscles relaxing, though adrenaline still pulsed through him.

Carmella stepped forward, her eyes wide with a mix of awe and fear. "That was… incredible. But are you okay?"

"Just doing what needed to be done," he replied, a hint of a smile breaking through. "As the saying goes, fuck around and find out. And they did."

Bane chuckled, clapping Damien on the back. "Ye never fail tae impress, Dame. But let's no' make a habit o' scaring our customers awa', aye?"

Damien surveyed the club. The patrons were still recovering from the shock, a mix of fear and admiration in their eyes. He had made his point—one that would echo through the supernatural community.

"Tonight, we protected our own," he said, his voice firm. "And anyone who thinks they can challenge that will face the fucking consequences."

With that, he straightened, the weight of his responsibilities settling back onto his shoulders. The night was still young.

"Next round is on the house." Music and the low hum of chatter started back up. "Let's get a quick cleanup before the band starts." This would feed the gossip mill about him, but he didn't give a shit.

The safety of his family and friends would always be his first priority, and he would ensure it remained that way, no matter the cost.

# Chapter 4

It was nearly midnight, but the moonlight bled through her picture window, casting a silver glow over the couch where Sadie sat—had been sitting for the better part of two hours.

Her tea had gone cold, but even if it had been hot, it wouldn't have been able to warm the ice that had settled in her bones. Tonight carried the crushing weight of eight years under Donovan's suffocating grip.

Eight years. The number clawed at her mind like a beast demanding acknowledgement. How could she be twenty-five when it seemed like yesterday she'd been seventeen, trembling in the backseat of his black sedan as he drove her toward what he'd called her "new beginning"?

Her fingers traced the rim of her untouched teacup, the porcelain smooth and cold beneath her touch. Every elegant curve of it whispered the same truth, his money, his choice, his control. She wanted to hurl it against the wall, watch it shatter into a thousand pieces, but destruction wouldn't change the chains that bound her to him.

Her gaze swept across the apartment she'd decorated with such care. Rugs she'd selected, paintings she'd chosen, furniture she'd arranged—all paid for with bills that bore his fingerprints. Even the salary deposited into her account each month flowed from his empire of shadows and secrets.

Her car? His generosity.

Her education? His investment.

Her livelihood? His leash.

Her entire existence revolved around Donovan Caine—drug dealer, criminal mastermind, and the puppet master who pulled her strings with surgical precision.

In exchange, she surrendered her gift, her curse, whenever he crooked his finger. She became his beck-and-call girl, his Friday night entertainment, his weekend weapon—available every hour of every day, no matter how her soul screamed in protest.

To his credit, Donovan wasn't entirely without mercy. Glimpses of humanity flickered behind his calculating eyes— rare moments when his laughter held genuine warmth instead of razor-sharp edges. But those flashes vanished as quickly as they appeared, leaving her wondering if she'd imagined them entirely.

She'd never felt the full force of his wrath, had never been the primary target when his temper erupted like a volcano. Disappointing him was punishment enough—the way his jaw tightened, how his voice dropped to that deadly whisper that made grown men wet themselves. So she danced to his tune, told him what he wanted to hear, even when it required weaving truth with carefully crafted lies.

Fabric, metal, stone, skin—nothing escaped the relentless pull of the past. History clung to objects like perfume, saturating them with memories that demanded to be witnessed. The good, the horrific, the soul-crushing truth—none of it cared whether she was ready to receive its secrets.

A whisper of contact was all it required. Her fingertips against any surface that had absorbed human emotion, and the world dissolved around her. She couldn't fully control the visions, but her skill at navigating them had sharpened over the years.

Psychometry—that was the clinical term Donovan had provided after funding research into her abilities. Before him, she'd been just another unwanted child rotting in the Sisters of Saint Vincent's Home, abandoned at age two by a mother whose face she couldn't even remember. Foster families had shuffled her from house to house like a contaminated package, terrified of a girl who convulsed and spoke to empty air about things that had happened decades before her birth.

At fifteen, she'd chosen the streets over another rejection. Those first months had been brutal—a teenage girl with no family, no resources, nothing but her wits and an uncontrollable gift that made her seem insane. But she'd adapted, survived, even found a lifeline in Maya, who volunteered at a girls' shelter just blocks from the infamous Wilshire Boulevard corner.

They exchanged occasional texts now and then. Careful messages that revealed nothing substantial. Sadie had learned early that closeness bred curiosity, and curiosity led to questions she could never answer. Her circle of trust was deliberately small—Donovan preferred it that way, though he never voiced his approval of her isolation.

Which explained why she spent Friday night alone in her apartment, working instead of living.

Donovan had acquired a collection of rare coins that afternoon, his voice carrying an undertone she'd learned to recognize over the years. This wasn't just another appraisal—it was an examination, a test wrapped in the guise of routine work. He'd requested she handle each piece, extract whatever historical value might increase their worth on the black market.

But Sadie knew he was hunting for something specific. The way his eyes had lingered on the small chest, the careful casualness of his instructions, everything screamed deception. Whatever truth these objects held, he already suspected it. He simply wanted to see if she'd be honest when she found it.

That's why her tea sat untouched, growing colder by the minute. The gold doubloons had pulled her centuries into the past, forcing her to witness men drowning in icy waters as their ship cracked apart in a storm. But those coins were merely camouflage. The real treasure lay at the bottom of the chest— an emerald and gemstone brooch whose story had unfolded in her palm like a poisonous flower...

*The insignia on the carriage door gleamed in the dying light, its gold edges catching the last rays of sunset. Horses' hooves thundered against cobblestones, white froth marking their mouths as terror drove them beyond their limits. Death pursued them with relentless hunger, and the animals sensed it in their bones.*

*Screams shattered the evening air as one wheel struck a jagged stone, the impact sending shockwaves through the entire structure. The carriage groaned and swayed, its elegant frame never designed for such desperate speed. Inside, bodies crashed against velvet seats—two men and one woman, all fighting to maintain their grip as their world tilted toward chaos.*

*Then silence fell over the roadway like a burial shroud. A stench of fear and approaching violence thickened the air, and Sadie found herself trapped within the vision, her modern apartment fading until only the past remained.*

*Dread coiled in her throat like a serpent, because she knew—she always knew—how these stories ended.*

*"Milady, stay behind us. We'll get you home safely."*

*Black-garbed riders materialized from the shadows like demons conjured from hell itself. Their horses were as dark as midnight, their cloaks and hoods even darker. Cruel laughter rippled through their ranks as they surrounded the overturned carriage, their numbers doubling the small party they'd cornered.*

*"Milady..." The guardian's protective words died as his head separated from his shoulders, a death rider's blade completing its arc in one fluid motion. Then there were two.*

*But the woman refused to cower. She stepped around her remaining protector, her spine straight despite the carnage painting the stones red. Royal blood ran through her veins, and it showed in every deliberate movement.*

*"If you strike against me, know that the king will hunt you down like the dogs you are."*

*"M'lady, stay behind me." Her final guardian moved to shield her, but his loyalty cost him everything. An arrow pierced his eye, dropping him to the cobblestones as his lady gasped in horror.*

*A voice that would haunt Sadie's dreams spoke from beneath one of the dark hoods—the leader of this pack of killers, she realized.*

*"King Louis's reign ends tonight, starting with your death."*

The window to the past began fracturing, historical images splintering like broken glass until the vision released its hold on her consciousness.

Sadie's hands trembled as she set the brooch aside, her heart hammering against her ribs. She'd need to research before reporting to Donovan, but the woman's regal bearing and the historical context suggested Marie Antoinette or one of Louis's prominent mistresses. Either way, the brooch was worth a fortune—and Donovan knew it.

This had been a loyalty test wrapped in the pretense of appraisal work. He wanted to see if she'd lie, if she'd try to deceive him about the brooch's true value. It was the game they'd played for years, each testing the other's boundaries while pretending trust existed between them.

Because Donovan trusted no one, and in this, his paranoia served him well. Sadie had been playing both sides for longer than he suspected, and she was determined that her side would win.

*Chapter 5*

Damien's fingers raked through his dark hair as he sat across from his mother, each strand catching between his knuckles like barbed wire. The familiar ache pulsed behind his temples—the same headache that surfaced every time she dragged him down this particular road to hell.

"Look, Mother." His voice carried the weight of exhaustion, each word carefully measured to avoid the explosion building in his chest. "We have traveled this ground so many times that the earth beneath us has turned to dust. This will be the final time I speak of it."

His knuckles whitened around the arms of his chair. The leather creaked under the pressure, a sound that mirrored the grinding of his teeth. "I gave love a chance once upon a time, and do you know what love gifted me in return? Nothing but fucking despair."

The air in the room thickened, pressing against his lungs like a physical weight. Memories clawed at the edges of his consciousness—a nursery painted soft blue, tiny fingers wrapped around his thumb, the scent of baby powder that had once made him believe in forever.

"I loved Sophia with every breath in my body. I handed her my soul on a silver platter, and she used it to carve out my heart." His voice cracked, the sound raw and jagged. "She gave me hope—three months of pure, untainted joy watching our son grow stronger each day. Then she ripped it away like tissue paper."

He shot to his feet, the chair spinning behind him as rage and grief warred in his chest. "She murdered my baby boy. They paint me as the monster in their whispered stories, but she was the real demon walking among us."

His fist slammed against the mahogany desk, the impact sending papers scattering like frightened birds. **"I WILL NOT WALK THAT PATH OF DESTRUCTION AGAIN!"**

Across from him, Gaia's tears carved silver trails down her olive cheeks. Each droplet carried the weight of watching her son transform from a man capable of tenderness into this fortress of fury and pain. Her fingers trembled in her lap, ancient power thrumming beneath her skin—power that could erase his memories, steal away the agony that consumed him.

But erasing pain meant erasing love, and if Damien ever discovered her betrayal, she would lose him to something far worse than grief. She would lose him to the truth of what she'd stolen.

"Damien," she whispered, her voice carrying the tremor of a mother's breaking heart. "Let me share this burden. You were never meant to carry such darkness alone."

His jaw clenched until the muscle jumped beneath his skin. "This conversation has reached its grave, Mother. I have an empire to run, and this burden—this rage—it's all I have left of my son's memory."

The chair scraped against marble flooring as he rose, each movement sharp with barely contained violence. Without another word, he strode from the room, leaving his mother to weep for the man her boy used to be.

## The Nikolas Law Firm

Damien's office occupied the top floor of a gleaming tower that scraped the belly of the sky, its windows offering a panoramic view of the city he controlled with an iron fist. To the outside world, he was simply another high-powered attorney. Behind closed doors, he was so much more.

His law practice served as the perfect mask—legitimate on the surface, with tentacles that reached deep into the shadows where real power lived and breathed. Every contract he drafted, every case he argued, and every client he represented added another layer to his carefully constructed empire.

Bane shouldered through the door without knocking, balancing a steaming cup of coffee in one massive paw. The hellhound's presence filled the room like smoke, his grizzled features carved from centuries of loyalty and mischief. He dropped the mug onto Damien's desk with a solid thunk.

"Thought ya could use a cuppa before ya turn inta a right bastard fer da rest of da day, boss."

Damien's middle finger shot up in response, the gesture automatic and somehow comforting in its familiarity. Bane's belly laugh rumbled through the office like distant thunder, the sound carrying echoes of millennia spent at each other's sides.

Their bond had been forged in the fires of creation itself, when Damien's divine power had breathed life into clay and shadow to create the first hellhound. Bane had emerged fully formed, already grumbling about the temperature and demanding something stronger than brimstone to drink.

"Ya wanna talk about it?" Bane's Celtic accent wrapped around the words like aged whiskey, smooth despite its rough edges.

"Nah, don't wanna talk about it," Damien replied, his own accent slipping into the familiar rhythm of their shared centuries.

Bane's head shook with theatrical disappointment before another laugh burst from his chest. "Don't try ta be me, ya accent sucks worse than week-old fish."

Despite the storm clouds still gathering in his mind, Damien's mouth twitched upward. "Business, old friend. How did the meeting with Jack and his crew unfold? Did he embrace the terms I so graciously offered?"

Bane leaned back in his chair, the leather groaning under his weight. "Ya know da stubborn prick didn't wanna sign. But Levi's powers of persuasion were... impressive, boss."

Damien arched one dark eyebrow. "Should I be concerned about the methods employed?"

A wicked grin split Bane's weathered features. "Does a hellhound piss fire?"

"I'm assuming that translates to 'yes' in your colorful vernacular?"

"Ya know I piss fire, so da answer is yes." Bane produced a rolled contract from his jacket, tossing it into the air and catching it with theatrical flair before waving it under Damien's nose. Jack's signature sprawled across the bottom in black ink, accompanied by a crimson thumbprint that spoke of ancient oaths sealed in blood.

Relief settled into Damien's shoulders, tension releasing like steam from a pressure valve. "Excellent. No illegal drugs flow through my territory—not in, not out, not even passing through on their way to someone else's nightmare. Jack understands that breaking this covenant means Bane personally escorts him to the deepest pits of hell, where he'll burn until the stars grow cold."

"Da bloody thumbprint seals da deal. Though Enzo threatening to cut off his manhood probably helped convince him da terms were reasonable."

Damien's laughter erupted, genuine and warm, the first real joy he'd felt since entering his mother's house that morning. "Enzo may be completely unhinged, but his loyalty runs deeper than blood. Come on, let's find the boys and drink to another successful negotiation."

# Chapter 6

"Sadie, wear the black dress to the gala tonight, if you please." Donovan's deep voice carried across his office as his scarred brow lifted—a gesture that said he expected no argument.

"Of course, Donovan." She turned toward the door, her shoulders already tensing as the familiar weight of his office pressed against her chest like a heavy blanket.

"Sadie?" Her name rolled off his tongue like honey laced with poison. Ice flooded her veins as she froze mid-step. "Once the event is underway, you'll escort me back into the museum's antiquities area. You can show me firsthand what you do on your days there."

Her stomach dropped. There it was—the real reason he'd suggested attending with her. Donovan always had an ulterior motive lurking beneath his generous offers.

Her part-time position at the Natural History Museum of L.A. had fallen into her lap because of him. It was a dream job. Anyone worth their credentials would kill for a position within those walls. She caught the sideways glances from other staff members—their eyes tracing her young face, her recent graduation date, their lips pressing together in thin lines of disapproval. She could practically hear their whispered assumptions: *She got the job on her knees.*

That would have been easier, she thought, her jaw clenching.

But Donovan had spotted her weakness like a predator sensing wounded prey. He'd dangled the opportunity in front of her, and she'd lunged for it, that persistent voice in her head whispering that she was sinking deeper into quicksand with each desperate grab.

School had come naturally to Sadie when she'd actually been able to attend. Bouncing from one foster home to another had left gaps in her education like missing teeth. When she'd finally run away at sixteen, choosing the streets over another failed placement, she'd carried only a ninth-grade education and a backpack of bruises.

Then Donovan had swept in, cape practically billowing behind him. He'd played her like a violin, and she'd let herself be tuned. Private tutoring in the mornings while she ran his mysterious errands each afternoon. Her high school diploma arrived in record time. He'd even thrown her a graduation party, renting out a small Greek restaurant complete with a house band that played traditional melodies while the scent of lamb and oregano filled the air.

The celebration had been intimate—just her, Donovan, and a handful of his other employees, since family was a word that didn't exist in her vocabulary. That night, as the last guest filtered out and only his security detail remained in the shadows, he'd presented her with a gold bracelet that caught the restaurant's warm lighting like captured starlight.

"Sadie, would you like to go further? College, maybe?"

The world tilted beneath her feet. College was a foreign concept—something for normal kids with normal families and normal lives. She was a system kid, a runaway, a freak who saw the past when she touched certain objects.

"You'd do that for me?" The words tumbled out before she could catch them, her excitement beating against her ribs like a caged bird.

Donovan waited until the restaurant grew quiet, until it was just them and the bodyguards positioned near the exits.

"I would. You're an asset to me and my business. As long as you agree to continue our arrangement."

Their arrangement. The phrase sat between them like a loaded gun. Using her gift of psychometry, however, he demanded. Carrying packages to locations he specified without asking questions. Loyalty to him and him alone.

"You wish to study history, yes?"

Her gaze snapped to his face, and in that moment, she felt the trap spring shut around her again.

Her gift had cracked open doorways to worlds she'd only read about in books. At the slightest touch of an object, Sadie could be hurled back centuries or further. The visions terrified her, yet they drew her in like a moth to flame, offering her a front-row seat to history's greatest dramas.

Some were horrific emotions that clung to her for days afterwards, interrupting her sleep with phantom screams and the metallic taste of ancient blood. But the experiences had ignited a hunger for knowledge, a desperate need to understand different cultures and historical civilizations.

Three years later, her B.A. hung framed on her apartment wall, and she possessed everything she'd never dared dream of. She should have been happy. Part of her was, the part that remembered being abandoned on the orphanage steps, a daughter so unwanted that even her own mother had walked away.

So what if her life came with strings attached? Didn't everyone owe someone something?

A warm touch at her hip yanked her from her thoughts. She looked up to meet Donovan's magnetic blue eyes—eyes that could convince saints to sin.

"It's time, Sadie. Let's take a walk." His hand pressed against her waist, guiding her toward the grand ballroom's entrance where tonight's event pulsed with classical music and clinking champagne glasses. Her simple black gown, sheer and form-fitting, offered no protection against the heat radiating from his palm.

Donovan rarely touched her. But lately, his hands had begun wandering—brushing her shoulder as he passed, grazing her arm during conversations, lingering longer than necessary.

Patrons nodded as they exited into the hallway, Donovan's recognizable face drawing second glances that included her by association. He was a frequent donor to the museum and other charitable events—a perfect mask for the shadows that followed him everywhere.

His breath tickled her ear as he leaned close, sending shivers down her spine. "Let's see what hidden gems we can find among all those artifacts in the back rooms, and what stories go with them, my sweet Sadie."

No one would question their departure. No one would wonder why they'd abandoned the music and dancing. Donovan Caine existed beyond approach, and by extension, so did she.

The museum's artifact wing would be deserted, everyone involved with the institution was currently sipping wine and making small talk at the gala. As Sadie lifted her hand to the keypad, her fingertip entering the code that would grant them access to the chambers housing unprocessed artifacts, she realized it would be just the two of them. She hesitated as the familiar electronic beep granted them entry.

"Sadie?" His hand squeezed her waist with gentle firmness.

She forced one foot in front of the other. The door clicked shut behind them with the finality of a coffin lid. Overhead fluorescent lights hummed to life, illuminating their path toward the work tables at the back of the facility.

She was crossing another line because of Donovan. Her stomach churned with the familiar weight of wrongdoing, but here she stood, as much a fraud and criminal as he was.

Their footsteps echoed off every surface, amplified like gunshots in a cathedral. Logic told her they wouldn't get in trouble, but her nerves screamed that alarms would blare at any moment.

"The artifacts we were working on today are still out in the back room if you want to see them." She gestured toward the general work area, hoping to steer Donovan away from the restricted vault—a violation that would feel exponentially worse than their current trespass.

"That's a start, then. Lead the way." His expression appeared genuinely interested, but with Donovan, masks were his speciality.

Two turns brought them to where she'd spent hours earlier that day. Sadie truly loved uncovering the history embedded in every item that found its way to their museum. Hidden secrets and untold stories clung to each piece like invisible fingerprints. She could live in these back rooms and find perfect contentment, though that remained a fantasy.

"I saw on the manifest that some items were uncrated yesterday. Is this what all this is?" His fingers traced the table's edge as his gaze moved from one artifact to another like a predator cataloging prey.

"Some of it. Other pieces went straight into the vault until we can assess them properly."

Donovan stopped and turned, his attention shifting toward the restricted area she desperately wanted to keep him away from. Without thinking, Sadie grabbed the nearest item from the display table—an ornate iron key. The moment her bare skin made contact with the metal, she knew she was about to be thrown backwards through time. There was no escape as the years began spinning her into the past...

*The stench hit her first—feces and urine so thick and heavy they seemed to coat her throat. Her hand flew up to cover her mouth and nose as inky blackness surrounded her, throwing off her balance. She couldn't distinguish up from down, left from right.*

*A low, dragged-out moan of pure agony echoed from somewhere to her left, raising every hair on her arms. Then came the sound of a door grating against stone, its unearthly creaking accompanied by flickering torchlight that cut through her peripheral vision. The flame grew brighter, steadier, as someone mounted it in a wall sconce.*

*Her eyes adjusted slowly, revealing what appeared to be a root cellar, though "dungeon" seemed more accurate. The floor consisted of hardened dirt and rock, slick with moisture that reflected the torchlight. In the far corner, that dancing flame illuminated a figure hanging from shackles around his wrists, suspended above the ground by chains anchored to the ceiling.*

*At least she thought it was a man. So disheveled and beaten, he resembled more beast than human. His moans filled the space again as she noticed the glint of metal around his throat—a collar that caught the light like a band of stars.*

*The creaking sound moved directly behind her as a hooded figure glided past, approaching the prisoner with predatory grace.*

*"This foolishness stops today. You will tell us where you hid the key, or by God's blood, I will spill the rest of yours onto this floor."*

*Panic clawed at Sadie's chest. She needed release from the vision's iron grip. "Please, please," she chanted silently, begging the past to relinquish its hold.*

*A blade emerged from the folds of the dark-robed figure's garments, its edge catching the torchlight like liquid silver. She tried to tear her gaze away, to close her eyes, but the unspoken rule of her gift held firm—the vision controlled her, not the other way around.*

*Slowly, the scene began fracturing around the edges. Her last sight was the blade striking the hanging man's flesh, his scream echoing through time...*

The window to the past slammed shut, leaving Sadie gasping and disoriented. She focused on deep breaths, trying to recenter herself while the weight of the key pressed against her palm like a burning coal, still trying to tell its story whether she wanted to hear it or not.

"Sadie, are you alright? What did you see?"

How much time had passed? It varied with each vision. At least she hadn't seized—a small mercy. Why had she grabbed the artifact without gloves? She knew better. Because she'd been desperate to distract Donovan from venturing deeper into the restricted areas.

Who was the man hanging in that medieval cell, and why had he been willing to die rather than reveal his secret? What did the key unlock, and had its contents ever been discovered? Sometimes she never received answers. Sometimes, all she gained was heartache. Gifts weren't supposed to inflict such pain.

"It was nothing of value, Donovan. Just an old man in great pain."

"Then let's continue our walk, Sadie."

# Chapter 7

Enzo knocked on Damien's office door before letting himself in. For the past few months, he'd diligently tracked Donovan Caine and a handful of other local thugs who operated under the radar. Damien wanted every detail: closest associates, dirty deeds, and where they laid their heads at night.

Donovan was notorious for slipping through fingers like smoke, always one step ahead of consequences. He'd throw his own mother under the bus to save his skin, leaving a trail of wreckage in his wake. Lately, his shadow had begun creeping into Damien's territory—an unwelcome intrusion that set Damien's teeth on edge.

Damien ran a tight ship and wouldn't tolerate anyone waltzing into his town to upset the delicate balance he'd bled to maintain. Whispers painted Donovan as a man of many trades: antiquities, cars, real estate—anything that lined his pockets and kept his fingers in the right pics. But the underground operations were what had Damien's hackles raised. Rumors of cutthroat tactics and blood money had a way of finding his ears.

Donovan had haunted L.A. for years, usually smart enough to stay invisible. But recently, he'd grown bold—or stupid. One thing Damien despised more than betrayal was a liar who thought himself untouchable. Time to discover exactly what Donovan Caine was selling, and if necessary, shut him down permanently.

Enzo wasn't just one of Damien's closest allies—he was one of the few vampires whose company Damien could stomach. The man could excavate secrets buried deeper than Jimmy Hoffa, navigating the dark web like its shadows pulsed through his veins.

"So what did you uncover, Enzo? How many businesses is he puppeteering, and who's dancing to his tune?"

Enzo placed the folder on Damien's desk with deliberate precision, the sound slicing through the silence like a blade. Photographs scattered across the mahogany surface, ex-convicts, desperate souls teetering on the razor's edge of legality. At the web's center sat Donovan: owner of two gentleman's clubs, a casino, and countless rental properties. His influence stretched like a cancer through the city's veins.

One photograph snagged Damien's attention. A striking blonde with eyes the color of warm caramel—Sadie Reed. Something in her gaze spoke of storms weathered and scars hidden beneath silk. He pulled her file closer, absorbing details of an orphanage childhood, a past that seemed to haunt the curve of her smile.

"Knew you'd fixate on her, boss." Enzo's mouth quirked upward. "Beautiful, sure, but there's steel beneath that porcelain exterior. The way she moves—like someone who's learned to expect the worst but hopes for better."

"There's something about her," Damien murmured, his voice dropping to a dangerous register. "What else did you dig up?"

Enzo leaned forward, a conspirator to the king. "Visited the museum where she works. Watched her handle artifacts like they were made of spun glass and dreams. When I struck up a conversation, her walls shot up faster than prison gates. But mention those ancient relics, and she transformed—passion bleeding through every word. She's human, no supernatural static, just someone searching for her place in a world that's chewed her up before."

Damien's interest sharpened. "How does she fit into Donovan's game?"

"Still piecing that puzzle together." Enzo's brow furrowed. "But she's deeper in than she realizes. Saw Donovan there once—schmoozing everyone like he owned the place. Calls himself a benefactor, which reeks of bullshit from where I'm sitting. There's something fragile about her that doesn't match the company she keeps."

Damien shook his head, knowing Enzo's poetic tendencies. "You know you're married, right?" he asked with dark amusement. "Is this how you seduced your wife—drowning her in flowery observations?"

Enzo's eyes glinted with mischief. "Love is a delicate dance, my friend. Poetry is merely one step in the choreography."

"A dance?" Damien's eyebrow arched. "How... romantic of you."

Enzo's smile turned predatory. "My wife wasn't easily impressed. She'd endured her share of suitors bearing grand gestures and hollow promises."

"And your secret weapon was what—sonnets?"

"Letters," Enzo confessed, his voice softening. "Not just any letters, poems. Each word selected like ammunition, each line aimed straight at her heart."

Damien laughed despite himself. "Poetry conquered the unconquerable?"

"Passionate verses about moonlit promises and stolen moments," Enzo's voice dropped to honey. "She fell for words that wrapped around her like silk."

"You calculating bastard."

"It worked." Enzo's expression grew earnest. "She surrendered to language that embraced her like a lover's touch."

Damien studied his friend's face. "What if she'd hated poetry?"

Sadness flickered across Enzo's features. "Then I would've found another key to her heart. Love isn't confined to rhyme or rhythm; it transcends every boundary we build."

"So love is poetry?"

Enzo's eyes sparked with hidden fire. "Love is the most devastating poem ever written."

Damien's expression hardened back to business. "I'm thinking Sadie doesn't realize the quicksand she's stepped into. With someone like Donovan, it's easy to mistake poison for wine until it's burning down your throat."

Enzo nodded, reading the shift in atmosphere. "Liability or asset?"

"Potential weapon," Damien replied, his mind already calculating angles. "If she's as passionate about those artifacts as you observed, she might stumble onto information that reveals more than Donovan intended. We keep her close."

"I'll shadow her movements," Enzo said, determination bleeding into his voice. "If she starts digging where she shouldn't, we intervene before she disappears permanently."

"Exactly." Urgency sharpened Damien's tone. "Find out what she knows and how deep Donovan's hooks are in her. If she's caught in his web, we extract her before she becomes another casualty."

# Chapter 8

Tears threatened the corners of her eyes—not from sadness, but from disgust with herself. She'd traveled so far down this criminal road with Donovan that every exit ramp had vanished in her rearview mirror. Now she was trapped on a one-way express to hell, with him gripping the wheel.

"Sadie, have you seen the two cylinders we set aside yesterday for examination? I'm certain I secured them in the vault before leaving." Mrs. Kendrick's usually immaculate chignon showed signs of her distress, silver strands escaping as her hand worried the back of her neck like a rosary.

"Sorry, I haven't seen them. I was buried in cataloging last week's collection of texts that Roger finished assessing. Maybe someone else moved them?" Sadie forced concern into her voice while her stomach churned with lies.

She projected professional calm while her insides performed gymnastics. The cylinders weren't just moved—they'd vanished. Gone from the museum, transported to God knows where, and her fingerprints were all over the crime.

She'd been Donovan's accomplice in what he'd sweetly called an "acquisition" while the gala provided perfect cover.

Still naive after all these years. "Donovan, surveillance blankets every inch of this museum, especially back here." But he'd already been three steps ahead, using her position like a chess piece he'd been maneuvering for months. How had she been so blind? She really was every blonde joke rolled into one pathetic package.

"Sadie, do you think I'd gamble with such amateur moves? Their security is child's play compared to my resources. Don't let worry steal that beautiful smile. I'd never let harm find you. Now, be my good girl and retrieve those paintings."

And she had been his good girl, extracting them from their climate-controlled sanctuary with the reverence of a tomb robber. One of Donovan's personal shadows materialized from thin air, accepting the artifacts with instructions on their handling and final destination. Then, as if nothing had transpired, Donovan's palm pressed against her spine, guiding her back into the crowd where champagne found her trembling fingers.

She'd drunk on an empty stomach because disappointment in herself tasted better than sobriety.

"I'm going to lose my job." Mrs. Kendrick's voice cracked, dragging Sadie back to the present nightmare.

The suggestion clawed up Sadie's throat before she could stop it. "Did anyone check the security footage? The cameras record continuously." Her lunch was performing a back pedal, threatening to make an appearance.

"Mr. Alexander reviewed everything the moment I mentioned the missing cylinders. The tapes show nothing suspicious. It's as if they simply evaporated, but I was the last person to handle them." Mrs. Kendrick's composure crumbled with each word.

---

Two hours and twenty-seven minutes later, Sadie navigated LA's arteries toward Donovan's casino. Thursday meant business meetings—heads of his various enterprises gathering around cards and calculations. She avoided eye contact with his associates, focusing solely on Donovan as her heels clicked across marble toward the blackjack table. The mountain of chips before him suggested fortune was on his side.

"Sadie, to what do I owe this unexpected pleasure?" All eyes swiveled toward her, but hers remained locked on his. The furrow between his brows telegraphed his displeasure at her unannounced arrival, but fear had wrapped cotton around her brain.

"I need a moment. It's important." The word "please" escaped like a prayer.

She'd never used that word with him before. The surprise flickered across his features.

"Gentlemen, excuse me briefly." His gaze shifted over her head. "Drake, refresh their drinks."

His imposing frame crowded her space as his hand claimed her hip—that same possessive grip from the night before— steering her toward doors marked "Staff Only." His access code granted entry to a concrete stairwell where her spine met a cold wall.

"Now tell me what drove you to seek me here, ma petite?"

"The museum discovered that the cylinders are missing. Mrs. Kendrick thinks she'll lose her job, or worse. Only a handful of us have access codes to that vault." She paused, drawing breath to steady herself, but Donovan had closed the distance while she spoke. Trapped, her hand rose instinctively to stop his advance, palm flattening against his chest. "The security footage shows nothing from last night. How is that possible? What did you do?"

She knew she was crossing lines drawn in his blood, but self-hatred made her reckless.

His hand covered hers, trapping it against his heartbeat. "Sadie, by tomorrow morning, those cylinders will resurface, looking carelessly misplaced with the paintings nestled inside. Stop torturing yourself. I'll never allow harm to touch you. You'll authenticate the paintings as originals, and this becomes ancient history."

His words struck wrong notes, discord ringing through her mind as his body caged her against the stone.

"What do you mean, no one will know what?" Her head tilted, catching the predatory gleam in his eyes—that familiar darkness she'd glimpsed before but chosen to ignore.

"The forgeries are masterpieces themselves. I paid handsomely for work beyond reproach. The counterfeiter needed weeks to perfect them for the gala, but timing aligned beautifully. Tomorrow you'll confirm their authenticity, and life continues."

Weeks. He'd orchestrated this elaborate dance for weeks while she'd been stumbling through steps she didn't know she was performing. She was a mere tool to him and she needed to keep reminding herself of that.

His hand released hers as he stepped back, voice sharpening like a blade. "Do we have a problem, Sadie?"

"No, of course not, Donovan. I'm glad you achieved your goal."

She steeled her expression into porcelain indifference, meeting his stare without flinching. His curt nod preceded his movement toward the exit. Code entered, door cracked, he paused. "Follow the stairs down, exit through the side door. We'll discuss this later." Then he vanished, leaving her to exhale relief into her tortured lungs.

He really was a monster. She needed to tattoo that truth onto her soul, a daily reminder carved in scar tissue. At least no one would lose their position, and her work could continue. She genuinely loved the museum. But how could she live knowing the destruction she'd enabled?

Then inspiration struck like lightning. If she examined those paintings, her touch might reveal the forger's signature— psychic fingerprints left in brushstrokes and pigments. If her abilities uncovered that information, she'd possess ammunition for whatever battle lay ahead. She already knew where several bodies were buried in Donovan's empire. Perhaps she was evolving, growing ruthless.

After all, she'd learned from a master.

*Chapter 9*

Damien's fingers drummed against the mahogany bar as questions churned through his mind. What invisible chains bound Sadie to that toxic bastard Donovan? His jaw clenched. Whatever secrets or leverage Donovan wielded, they kept her trapped in his web like a fly waiting to be devoured.

Yet something about her pulled at him—a magnetic force he couldn't name. He wanted to peel back her layers, understand what drove her, maybe even throw her a lifeline out of whatever hell she'd fallen into.

His phone buzzed. Another text from Bane: *Still watching. No movement yet.*

Each surveillance report only twisted the knot in his chest tighter.

He glanced at his watch and exhaled slowly. The Egyptian artifact should arrive any minute now—Kimora's birthday surprise. The shabtis had taken weeks to track down, but the joy that would light up her face when she unwrapped it? Worth every connection he'd called in and every dollar he'd spent.

The irony wasn't lost on him. His investigation into Donovan's museum connections had sparked the idea for Kimora's gift. Her own Egyptian heritage made it perfect—something from her past, a bridge to her ancestors.

His Italian leather shoes scraped against the floor as he paced Enigma's dimly lit interior. The bass from the sound system thrummed through his chest, but it did nothing to settle his restless energy. Waiting made his skin crawl.

When he'd contacted the L.A. Museum, they'd passed him up the chain like a hot potato—director to board member to the deep pockets who made things happen. A sizable donation later, and the shabtis was his.

But Damien had played chess long enough to think three moves ahead. Donovan spent considerable time at that museum. The moment word reached him about a private purchase and generous donation, his curiosity would spike. And if the buyer was Damien Nikolas? The bastard would insert himself into the delivery personally. Had to meet the man behind the money.

Sure enough, the email confirmed it: one of their "generous benefactors" would handle the delivery personally.

Damien's lips curved into a predatory smile. Donovan Caine, you predictable piece of shit.

Finally, he'd meet his enemy face-to-face. Years of reading people had honed his instincts to a razor's edge, and he couldn't wait to see just how deep Donovan's corruption ran. Already, he suspected it was the kind of filth that stuck to your shoes after walking through a sewer.

The club's heavy door swung open, and relief flooded through him—

Then stopped cold.

Sadie.

Her golden hair caught the amber glow of the bar lights as it cascaded over her shoulders. Delicate features emerged from the shadows as she walked toward him, and he drank in every graceful step.

Then her scent hit him.

Demon.

The smell clung to her skin like smoke, making his nostrils flare and his hands curl into fists. Another male's essence marked her, and it sent something feral clawing up his throat. His monster stirred beneath his skin, recognizing a threat, a rival.

Did she know what Donovan really was? Had she sold her soul to him?

He forced his breathing to steady, his face to remain neutral. Not here. Not now. But this chance encounter just became infinitely more valuable. Time to discover what dark bargains bound her to that demon.

She slid onto a barstool, cradling a wooden box against her chest. So Donovan was too much of a coward to face him directly. Interesting.

Damien's grin spread wide as he set a crystal tumbler before her, ice clinking against the sides. "I wanted to thank you, Sadie." Her name rolled off his tongue likc honey. "Your prompt delivery means everything. This gift will make a dear friend's birthday unforgettable."

Her brow furrowed, confusion flickering across her features. He could practically see the gears turning—How does he know my name? What has Donovan told him about me?

The uncertainty hung between them like morning fog. Her fresh, sweet scent underneath the demon's stench made his body respond in ways that had nothing to do with territorial anger and everything to do with want.

But then her cute button nose wrinkled in distaste. She pushed back from the bar, chair legs scraping against the floor. "I was just doing my job."

Without another word, she stood and headed for the exit, her heels clicking against the hardwood like a countdown.

Something twisted in his chest as he watched her retreat. He replayed their brief exchange—he hadn't been his usual abrasive self. He'd been genuine, even warm. So why was she running like he'd threatened her?

"Why don't you join me for the birthday celebration?" His voice carried over the music. "You look like you could use some fun."

---

"Donovan, couldn't one of the boys handle this delivery? I really wanted to get back to the museum for a few hours." Sadie already knew the answer, but she had to try.

"Sadie." His eyes shifted to a more hazel hue, and the full weight of his attention settled on her like a heavy blanket. "If I remember correctly, I'm the boss. But I'm not asking as your employer—I'm asking as your friend. We are friends, aren't we?"

Her stomach sank as she nodded. Friend. What a joke. You didn't say no to Donovan Caine, period. But lately, the urge to push back grew stronger each day. His leash seemed to tighten around her neck weekly, questioning where she went, who she saw, and even having his security tail her.

"Good." His smile held no warmth. "The museum sold one of the shabtis pieces to a private buyer. Since you're our historian, and he might have technical questions, you're the perfect escort."

Her eyebrows drew together as she stared at the narrow lockbox on his desk. "One of the pieces from the Penn museum exchange? Those were for sale?"

The exhibit swap had been one of the few bright spots in her recent work. Museums struggled to stay relevant in the digital age, but the Egyptian collection still drew school groups and tourists.

"If you're asking if it's legal?" His tone sharpened. "It is. Mr. Damien Nikolas paid fair market value, and all documentation follows Egyptian antiquities law. So wipe that worry off your face." He pushed off from his desk, closing the distance between them. "You'll deliver the box and authentication letter."

She tried not to flinch. At least half his business dealings lived in gray areas at best, so her caution wasn't unfounded.

"Give me the address, and I can drop it off on my way home."

But he was already moving, stopping directly in front of her. His fingers lifted a strand of her hair off her shoulder, the crisp scent of his aftershave invading her space. "Thank you, ma petite."

His lips brushed her cheek—light as a whisper, but it might as well have been a brand.

Sadie's body turned to stone. Her stiletto heels pressed into the low-pile carpet as if they could anchor her to the earth. He'd never kissed her before. Ever. Not even this barely-there peck.

She'd caught him watching her sometimes, that predatory gleam in his eyes making her skin crawl. But they'd always maintained professional boundaries. She was already drowning in his web—she didn't need him pulling her deeper.

Without meeting his eyes, she skirted around him and lifted the wooden box. Surprisingly light for something so ancient. She placed the envelope carefully on top. "I'll text you when it's delivered. See you tomorrow."

When she glanced back, he wore that expression she'd seen before—the cat with a mouse trapped between its paws.

She forced herself to walk, not run, to the door. Only when it clicked shut behind her did she allow herself a shaking breath.

---

Google Maps led her to a nightclub. At least it was late afternoon, so hopefully empty enough for a quick in-and-out delivery.

She took a moment in her car to search for the buyer's name. **Damien Nikolas.** Limited results, but she found a photo— intense eyes staring out from her phone screen.

Her pulse stuttered. **Wow.**

"Get it together," she muttered, grabbing her bag and the box. "Let's get this over with."

The door to Enigma opened to reveal low lighting, soft music, and—across the room's length—the buyer himself.

Even from this distance, his size was imposing. Not just tall but broad-shouldered, built like he could bench press a car. His stare pinned her in place, making each step forward feel like walking through quicksand.

By the time she reached the bar where he stood, her nerves were jangling like alarm bells. She perched on a stool and set the box between them, fighting the urge to fidget under his scrutiny.

His voice was velvet over gravel as he thanked her, sliding an unsolicited drink across the bar. The shabtis was a gift, he explained, for someone special.

But it was hearing her name from his lips that sent her composure scattering like leaves in a hurricane. She'd never met him before—she'd have remembered his face and presence. Maybe Donovan had called ahead.

The thought of someone treating a priceless artifact like a trinket made her jaw clench. These pieces deserved reverence, care, not to be passed around like party favors.

She slid off the stool and straightened her blazer. "I was just doing my job." The words came out sharper than intended. "If you have questions, call Donovan or the museum."

She made it three steps before his voice stopped her cold.

He wanted her to join them? For a party?

The words tumbled through her mind like Scrabble pieces, but no matter how she rearranged them, they formed the same impossible sentence.

She turned slowly, studying his face for signs he was joking. "Why would you ask me that? You don't know me. I don't know you. And I sure as hell don't know whoever's having this birthday."

Her gaze swept the empty club before returning to his. Waiting.

---

Damien read the tension in every line of her body, the way she held herself like a bird ready to take flight. Her hostility was a living thing between them, and he found himself genuinely curious about its source. Sure, Donovan was a manipulative bastard, but what had he told her about himself specifically?

"I thought it might be nice for you to have some fun without worrying about anything." He kept his voice gentle, non-threatening. "You could see the good home your delivery is going to, and enjoy some pleasant company."

She stood frozen, statue-still. Confusion painted her beautiful features as she searched for the perfect excuse to refuse. When was the last time someone offered her something without strings attached?

---

Maybe she'd hit her head and slipped into some alternate dimension. Considering her gift and the places it had yanked her into with just a touch, parallel universes weren't outside the realm of possibility.

The day had started wrong—Donovan's unusual familiarity, the way he'd cornered her, that kiss. Now Damien's intensity rolled off him in waves, his pale blue eyes tracking her every movement since she'd entered his domain. His voice was rough velvet, stroking along her nerves and adding to her unease.

Everything felt balanced on a knife's edge lately, like her whole life was held together with fraying thread. That sensation gripped her again as she stood halfway out the door, caught between flight and something she couldn't name.

She looked back at Damien, weighing her options. Lesser of two evils? She was supposed to text Donovan when the delivery was complete, but something about his behavior today made her want to stay unavailable for the rest of the night.

Her feet carried her back before her brain caught up. "This isn't a date." She met his eyes directly. "I want that crystal clear."

Somewhere in the dark corners, everyone pretended they didn't have disappointment flickered. She crushed it ruthlessly.

Then he smiled, and her body responded with embarrassing enthusiasm. **Down, girl.** Yes, he was attractive, but that came with a whole catalog of red flags. Arrogant. Entitled. And if he knew Donovan, definitely trouble.

She grabbed her traitorous hormones by the throat and shoved them back into their cage.

"I'm just going to freshen up." She needed distance, space to get her head screwed on straight.

In the restroom, she ran a comb through her hair and touched up her lip gloss, then pulled out her phone. A quick text to Donovan: Shabtis delivered safely. See you tomorrow.

She powered off the phone before he could respond. Let tomorrow worry about tomorrow.

Her reflection stared back from the mirror—flushed cheeks, bright eyes. This is stupid. But maybe, just maybe, meeting the artifact's new owner would ease her conscience about its care.

Keep telling yourself that, her reflection seemed to say.

---

Damien's smile spread across his face at the sound of her returning heels. He liked her fire, the challenge she presented. It had been too long since someone made him work for their attention.

"Blondie, we're definitely on the same page. This isn't a date—just two people getting to know each other and enjoying a party."

Fire flared in the caramel swirls of her eyes, and her words hit him like a physical blow somewhere south of his belt buckle.

"Don't call me Blondie. I have a name. Use it."

Something primitive stirred in his chest as she stalked past him toward the door—recognition from the monster he kept caged. This one, it whispered. This one is different.

---

Thirty minutes later, every head in the room turned as Damien and Sadie entered together. Bane's jaw actually dropped, his eyes widening as he took in Damien's unexpected plus-one.

"Wha dae ah have the pleashure o' meetin'?" Bane approached with his trademark grin, extending his hand. The hellhound's charm was legendary—few could resist those dimples.

Sadie hesitated for a heartbeat before accepting his handshake. "Hello. I'm Sadie. Pleasure to meet you."

Even she wasn't immune to Bane's magnetism, her posture relaxing slightly. "Ah, it's braw to meet ye as well, Sadie!"

"Let me introduce you to the others." Damien's hand found the small of her back, guiding her around the room. He wanted her comfortable, settled, before the inevitable interrogation began.

That's when he discovered Enzo could actually look guilty.

"Hello again, Sadie. Small world." Enzo's usual cockiness faltered. "I didn't know you and Damien were acquainted."

Sadie glanced up at Damien before responding. "We actually just met today. The world is vast yet small, isn't it? How do you two know each other?"

The look that passed between Damien and Enzo didn't escape her notice.

"He's the big boss man," Enzo shrugged. "He says jump, I sometimes ask how high. Depends on how nicely he asks."

"On that note, let's keep moving." Damien steered her away before Enzo could dig himself deeper. "He never knows when to shut up, and I don't want to listen to him jabber all night."

Odd, Sadie thought, but the notion fled as she was absorbed into the group of women.

Genevieve, Bristol, and Kimora descended on her like long-lost sisters, pulling her away from Damien with practiced ease. He recognized their looks—they wanted to interrogate the woman who'd put a genuine smile on their friend's face.

Kimora was sweetness personified, but threaten her family and she'd strike like a scorpion. Bristol had survived hell and come out swinging. Genevieve could charm secrets from a stone.

Damien's eyes tracked Sadie's every movement, the magnetic pull between them stronger than anything he'd felt in years. He liked it. Craved it.

"Nice to see you smile, boss." Enzo shook his head, chuckling. "Didn't think we'd ever see you bring another woman into our circle after what happened with your ex-wife."

Heat flashed through Damien's veins like lightning. He never wanted reminders of that woman, especially since she was the reason his son—

Sadie's laughter cut through his rising rage like sunlight through storm clouds. Rich, genuine, completely unguarded. Something in his chest settled, and then he immediately wanted more.

He was falling under her spell, and for the first time in years, he didn't want to fight it.

---

Walking into the party beside Damien, Sadie stopped so abruptly that his chest brushed her back. Every conversation halted, every eye turned their way. Am I underdressed? Probably, since this wasn't exactly planned. She should be home in sweats and pajama pants, eating Chinese takeout and binge-watching Friends.

The man who approached them—Bane, she learned—immediately pegged her as out of her element. His outstretched hand made her stomach clench. She usually avoided handshakes, stuck to fist bumps or kept her hands busy, but refusing would seem rude.

Please, she sent up a silent prayer. Just a normal handshake.

"I'm Sadie. Pleasure to meet you." She kept the contact light and brief, relief flooding her when no visions crashed through her skull.

From there, Damien stayed close as they circulated the room, her stealing hopefully subtle glances his way until the women claimed her.

Kimora, the birthday girl, pulled her aside after the initial introductions. "It's lovely to meet you. Damien told me you found such a rare artifact for my birthday. There's so much of my ancestors' history in it."

Her smile was infectious, and Sadie felt her shoulders drop from around her ears. "I delivered it to Damien"—her gaze found his across the room, already focused on her—"but I'd be happy to discuss its origin anytime. I work part-time at the Natural History Museum."

She deliberately avoided mentioning her other employer, not wanting to invite questions about Donovan.

The evening flew by faster than she wanted to admit. She found herself genuinely liking these people—their easy camaraderie, their obvious affection for each other. And Damien...

**Don't.** She couldn't afford to like him. Couldn't afford to notice how her pulse jumped when their eyes met across the room, or how her skin heated when he appeared beside her during conversations with other guests.

As Bane and Kimora thanked everyone for coming, Damien's breath tickled her ear. "I know this wasn't a date, but I hope we can do this again."

Her body swayed toward his before she caught herself. **Traitor**.

She steeled her spine and turned to face him, intending to make it clear this was a one-time thing. But looking up into his face, seeing something almost vulnerable in those intense eyes, different words escaped.

"Maybe."

# Chapter 10

The thought slammed into her consciousness the moment she woke the next morning, her eyes flying open. **Maybe**. She'd actually told Damien **maybe** to seeing him again. Her stomach twisted as she stared at the ceiling. What had she been thinking? That single word was like striking a match in a room filled with gasoline.

If Donovan discovered she was spending time with him... Her chest tightened. She'd witnessed Donovan's temper—the way his jaw would tick before the storm hit, how his voice dropped to that deadly whisper that made her blood run cold. And lately, something told her she hadn't even glimpsed the worst of what lived inside him.

The changes in Donovan had been subtle at first. His fingers would graze her arm as he passed, lingering just a heartbeat too long. His stare had grown heavier, more possessive, burning into her skin like a brand. The invisible clock in her chest ticked louder each day.

Eight years. Eight years of this suffocating existence, and her soul screamed that the end was finally approaching. Her anxiety had become a living thing, clawing at her ribs, whispering in an endless loop that she needed to escape his web before it was too late.

But Donovan wouldn't simply let her walk away—not with everything she knew about him and his empire. She'd been collecting pieces of information like breadcrumbs, storing them away for the day she might need them. Insurance. Because Donovan wore two faces, and she'd learned to fear them both.

The world saw the philanthropist, the successful businessman who donated millions to worthy causes. But she knew the truth lurking beneath that polished exterior. He commanded the west coast underground with ruthless precision, and by the time she'd realized the full extent of his power, his claws were already too deep.

So why today? Why was she finally admitting these truths to herself?

The answer made her breath catch. Pale blue eyes that seemed to see straight through her defenses. A voice like aged whiskey that poured warmth through her veins. Hands that had touched her so briefly yet left her entire body humming with need.

Damien. Even thinking his name sent heat spiraling through her core.

Donovan's fury would be volcanic. She couldn't explain how she knew, but the certainty sat heavy in her stomach. She wasn't actively searching for someone, but she'd always known that someday she might meet someone worth the risk. Donovan would have to understand that.

After all, she'd watched him parade countless women through his life over the years. Her own isolation hadn't been by choice—Donovan controlled every aspect of her existence, leaving no room for relationships or normalcy for her.

But things were different now. School was behind her. The museum work gave her purpose. She'd more than repaid whatever debt he claimed she owed him. The illegal activities he'd coerced her into, the moral compromises that still made her sick—she'd calculated the profits. Millions. Her debt was paid with interest.

She wanted simple things. The right to choose her own path. The freedom to explore whatever Damien had awakened inside her. But how could she claim those wants without igniting a war? Both men were forces of nature, and one wrong move would send them crashing into each other, with her caught in the middle.

More leverage. That's what she needed. Every scrap of information she could gather and hoard before making her move.

The vault's fluorescent lights hummed overhead as she made her way to Aisle 3, Row 2. The metal cylinders housing the forged paintings sat innocuously beside a box of ancient pottery. No one had any reason to disturb them—they'd been authenticated, catalogued, and filed away among hundreds of other artifacts.

She just needed a few minutes of contact.

The storage area felt colder today, though whether from the climate control or her nerves, she couldn't say. The museum maintained precise temperature and humidity levels to preserve their collection. Even the lighting posed a threat to delicate artifacts, which meant strict protocols—lights on when entering, off when leaving. Mrs. Kendrick had made that abundantly clear last week when she'd publicly dressed down poor Roger for his oversight.

**Focus.**

Her hands trembled as she lifted the pottery box's lid, angling her body to block the security camera's view. The ceramic pieces inside caught the light, their ancient surfaces holding stories she'd never need to touch to know.

But the metal cylinder called to her.

She unscrewed the cap carefully, then made a show of examining one of the pottery pieces, holding it where the camera could capture her innocent research. Her fabricated story sat ready on her tongue, though she prayed no one would ask.

After returning the pottery to its place, she steadied herself against the metal shelving and slipped her fingertips into the cylinder. The canvas felt cool beneath her touch.

The vision hit like a thunderclap.

Images cascaded through her mind, scattered photographs tumbling over each other in rapid succession. She'd learned to pay attention during these moments. There were never second chances or do-overs.

Numbers flashed: 621. A street sign reading Canon Drive. A glimpse of a house, a tabletop cluttered with objects moving too quickly to identify. Then the pace slowed, the image sharpening into focus—a face reflected in a mirror, features blurred but distinctive enough.

She jerked her fingers back, gasping.

Her mouth felt cotton-dry, but relief loosened the tension in her shoulders. That had been mercifully brief compared to some visions. She quickly screwed the cap back into place and spent several minutes memorizing the pottery collection, building her alibi.

The lights clicked off behind her as she stepped into the corridor.

"Sadie."

She stumbled, a shocked breath escaping her lips.

"Donovan." Her heart hammered against her ribs. "What are you doing here?"

She'd chosen this late afternoon hour specifically because most staff had gone home to dinner and family obligations.

"You know I have an investment interest in the museum." His footsteps echoed as he moved closer—one step, then two. "What were you doing in the vault? I thought you'd have left by now."

"I thought you were handling that business dinner tonight."

The words slipped out before she could stop them. Donovan's gaze locked onto her, and something shifted in his expression—something that made her blood turn to ice. His eyes seemed to darken, pupils disappearing into expanding pools of black.

"Sadie." Her name came out like a warning. "Don't play games with me. You've been testing boundaries lately, and I've been patient. But my patience has limits." His entire demeanor transformed, revealing the predator she'd always sensed lurking beneath his civilized mask. "I own you. Don't forget that. So I'll ask once more—what were you doing in there?"

Terror should have had her shaking, but somehow she remained steady under his predatory stare. This wasn't the first time recently he'd pinned her with that soul-piercing glare, as if he could read every thought in her head.

"I was examining the Incan pottery collection. I wanted to propose rotating the display in the second wing to the council. I was checking our available inventory."

The lie rolled off her tongue smoothly—she'd rehearsed it multiple times, preparing for exactly this moment. Anyone might question why she'd entered the vault when her current assignment involved scrolls housed in an entirely different section.

Donovan stood motionless, saying nothing. The silence stretched until her lungs burned from holding her breath.

Then, as casually as discussing the weather, he said, "Sadie, there's only one side to be on—mine. If I discover otherwise..." He paused, letting the threat hang in the air. "I will kill you."

He leaned forward and pressed a soft kiss to her forehead, the gesture obscenely gentle given his words. Then he simply... vanished. Not walked away—disappeared completely, as if he'd never been there at all.

She'd always known he was something more than human. Something that prowled in the darkness. And now she knew her time had run out.

Had she spoken Damien's name aloud, or only thought it? Could he help her, or should she just run?

She gathered her bag with trembling hands, forcing herself to move normally. "Stay calm. Act natural." Donovan had her followed before—he could be watching even now.

Five minutes later, she sat in her locked car, phone clutched in her hands. Before she could second-guess herself, she hit send on the message she'd typed:

**Damien, I'm in trouble.**

# Chapter 11

Dawn bled through the heavy curtains of Damien's penthouse, casting long shadows across marble floors that had witnessed more confessions than a cathedral. He stood sentinel at the floor-to-ceiling windows, jaw carved from granite as he watched the city stretch and yawn beneath him. Sleep had abandoned him hours ago, leaving him alone with thoughts that circled like vultures.

The weight pressed down on his shoulders—not just of an empire built on fear and respect, but of the careful balance he maintained between two worlds that would tear each other apart given half a reason. Today, that weight felt like carrying mountains.

Faces flickered through his mind like a deck of cards shuffled by a dealer with bloody hands. Each one represented today's meetings, each smile hiding fangs, each handshake a potential knife in the back. The careful threads of his network had been fraying lately, amateur hands pulling at strings they didn't understand, unraveling work that had taken decades to weave.

Did they really think he was blind?

The thought curved his lips into something that would have made angels weep. He'd been orchestrating this symphony of shadows since before most of these pretenders had drawn their first breath. Their clumsy attempts at manipulation were about to earn them a master class in consequences.

The beast stirred beneath his ribs, a restless hunger that had been denied too long. Years of betrayal had forged his heart in fires that would melt lesser metals, and today, someone would feel the full weight of what they had helped create.

His reflection stared back from the window—steel-blue eyes that had seen empires rise and fall, features carved by time and violence into something that belonged more in ancient marble than flesh. The arbiter of supernatural justice. The god of monsters. Whispered names that made hardened killers check their shadows twice.

A single nod to Enzo across the room. The Italian's dark eyes gleamed with understanding.

"Aye, boss, what's the plan for today then?" Bane's grin split his weathered face, dimples appearing like old friends. The anticipation in his green eyes spoke of shared battles and spilled blood.

Damien lifted the crystal tumbler to his lips, savoring the way the whiskey carved fire down his throat. When he set the glass down, it rang against marble like a death knell. His gaze swept his assembled crew—Bane with his Scottish fire, Enzo shadows made flesh, Levi prowling restlessness.

"We're paying Remus and his pack a visit." His voice carried the promise of storm clouds gathering. The smile that followed held winter's bite. "No pun intended, Levi."

The werewolf's answering chuckle rumbled like distant thunder.

Remus. The name left ash on his tongue. Months of pushing boundaries, testing the delicate equilibrium that kept their world from sliding into chaos. The arrogant bastard believed himself above the laws that governed them all, as if centuries of careful balance meant nothing compared to one wolf's wounded pride.

Today, that delusion died.

The laws weren't suggestions scrawled in some dusty tome—they were the foundation stones that prevented both worlds from crumbling into ash and screaming. One rogue wolf's reckless pride wouldn't be allowed to tip those scales toward disaster.

Enzo's hands flexed at his sides, nostrils flaring as if he could already taste violence on the morning air. "Nothing like the scent of battle to start the day right." His eyes held the hunger of predators who had been kept on too tight a leash. "Time to remind them who rules this city."

Reality rippled around them like water disturbed by thrown stones. The penthouse dissolved, marble and steel giving way to wood and morning light. They materialized in the heart of werewolf territory, where the scent of pack and wild things hung heavy in the air.

Remus sat at his breakfast table as if he'd been expecting them, fork suspended halfway to his mouth, utterly unfazed by their sudden appearance. The wolf's casual indifference stoked the flames higher in Damien's chest.

The fork clinked against porcelain as Remus set it down with deliberate slowness. He rose from his chair like a king granting audience, meeting Damien's stare with infuriating calm. His gesture toward the empty chairs held mock hospitality that made Damien's teeth ache.

"To what do I owe the honor of this unexpected visit, Damien?" The wolf's voice carried false warmth. "And you've brought friends."

Bane's chuckle rumbled through the tension. "Oh, ye've been more than a wee bit naughty, haven't ye, Remus?"

Patience—that virtue Damien had cultivated through centuries of negotiation and diplomacy—snapped like a chain under too much weight.

"Enough games." Each word fell like hammer blows. "You know exactly what you've done. The danger you've put us all in with your reckless stupidity."

He pointed an accusatory finger at the defiant wolf, letting every ounce of his authority bleed through. "Your tantrum ends today. Fall in line and respect the laws that bind us all, or face the consequences." His voice dropped to registers that made reality shiver. "I won't hesitate to burn you and your entire pack to ash if that's what it takes to restore order."

The words hung in the air like a death sentence, promising the storm about to break.

Enzo snapped his fingers with theatrical flair, winking as the breakfast room dissolved around them. "The Bataka battlefield seems more appropriate, don't you think, boss?"

Ancient stone rose from nothing, weathered by time and stained with the blood of ages. The scent of old battles filled the air—copper and smoke, victory and defeat mingled until they became indistinguishable. Damien surveyed the blood-soaked ground where countless warriors had fallen throughout history, adding their stories to the stones.

"I guess you've made your choice, Remus."

Across the constructed battlefield, Remus and his pack shed their human masks. Canines gleamed like ivory daggers in the morning light as they bared their fangs, fur bristling with aggression that rippled through the air like heat waves. The ground trembled beneath their combined growls, a bass note that spoke of wild places and older laws.

The battle erupted like a dam bursting.

Damien moved with the terrible grace of forces beyond nature—waves of monstrous energy rippling from his form, cracking stone and darkening sky. The very air bent to his will as he wielded power that could reshape reality itself. Enzo became the form of shadow and death, draining life with each precise strike, leaving desiccated husks where living beings had stood moments before.

Bane's flames roared to life, consuming everything in their path and reducing Remus's followers to ash and fading screams. Levi's growl harmonized with the werewolves' rage as his Lycan claws carved through fur and flesh, showing the mercy that came only through swift death.

Unity and centuries of experience proved stronger than reckless rebellion. The tide shifted inevitably in their favor, as it always had, as it always would. With a final, cataclysmic wave of energy, Damien swept the last of the resistance from the field— divine retribution made manifest in smoke and silence.

Dust settled on stones already stained with the blood of ages. The echoes of violence faded into memory, leaving only the whisper of wind through broken battlements. Damien and his crew stood victorious among the ruins, balance restored through necessary brutality.

The sun climbed higher, painting the aftermath in shades of gold and crimson that spoke of endings and beginnings. Damien turned to his companions, his eyes reflecting gratitude earned through shared bloodshed and unwavering loyalty.

"Thank you." The words carried the weight of centuries, of brotherhood forged in fire and sealed in blood. "Your loyalty is worth more than kingdoms."

His phone buzzed against his chest, and the world contracted to that single vibration. Sadie's name on the screen made his heart stutter against his ribs. The message turned his blood to ice water: **Damien, I'm in trouble**.

"Handle the cleanup," he told his crew, reality already bending around him like smoke.

The battlefield dissolved. Marble floors materialized beneath his feet, then faded. Stone steps, brick walls, wooden doors—all blurred past as he traveled between heartbeats, desperation lending speed to power that already defied comprehension.

He materialized outside Sadie's door, still wearing battle-like cologne—blood on his hands, violence clinging to him like a second skin. His fist connected with her door three times, sharp and urgent, each knock echoing his racing pulse.

The door swung open.

Sadie stood framed in the doorway, morning light catching the gold in her hair and turning it to spun sunbeams. Her eyes widened as she took in his appearance—the predator barely contained beneath his civilized mask, the evidence of what he was capable of written in crimson across his knuckles.

"D-Damien." His name fell from her lips like a prayer and a curse combined, relief and terror dancing in those storm-gray depths.

The battle-hardened exterior he wore like armor cracked the moment he saw her fear. Blood-stained hands rose to cup her face with infinite gentleness, thumbs brushing across cheekbones like she was made of spun glass. He searched her eyes for wounds that might not show, for the source of whatever had driven her to reach for him.

"Sadie, what's wrong? Are you hurt?" His voice carried vulnerability that few had ever witnessed—the monster showing his heart to the one person who could destroy him with a whispered word.

# Chapter 12

The ocean breeze carried salt through her open windows, but Sadie tasted nothing. Traffic lights blurred past—red, green, yellow—their colors meaningless as her hands moved the steering wheel without thought. Her exit appeared like a mirage, and somehow she was navigating familiar streets, muscle memory guiding her home while her mind remained trapped in the museum with Donovan's words echoing.

**Comply or die.**

The steering wheel creaked under her white-knuckled grip. Years of staying, of making excuses, of pretending she didn't notice the way shadows bent around him or how his staff moved with inhuman grace—it all crashed down at once. She should have run the first time she'd seen him materialize from thin air. Should have trusted the ice that crawled up her spine whenever he smiled in that certain way.

But could anyone really escape someone like Donovan? Someone who wasn't bound by human limitations? The word "supernatural" felt clumsy on her tongue, inadequate for whatever he truly was. She'd kept herself deliberately ignorant, afraid that knowledge would make her more of a target than her gift already did.

Her gift. The curse that let her touch objects and see their histories, feel the emotions embedded in them. It made her valuable to him—a living archaeological tool he could control with threats. The bitter irony wasn't lost on her: she could read the past of anything except her own future.

She'd thought maybe for a hot minute she could be otherworldly. Trying out that word, but it still felt wrong. But she wasn't. She could be killed and die like any human. And that was Donovan's leverage.

Her street sign materialized through the windshield haze. How did I get here without killing someone?

The townhouse complex stretched in neat rows, identical units with identical front steps. She parked and scanned the shadows between buildings, her heart hammering as she bolted from car to door. The key slipped in her sweaty fingers before finally turning, and she slammed the deadbolt home with a metallic click that sounded too loud in the silence.

Donovan had vanished right in front of her today—there one second, gone the next. If he could do that, locks meant nothing. Her apartment probably wasn't safe, had never been safe. Sometimes she'd catch traces of his cologne lingering in rooms when he hadn't been here, but she'd always convinced herself it was her imagination.

Her phone screen remained dark. No messages from Damien. He was probably busy, and this was her own mess anyway. She shouldn't have reached out to him. What the hell had she been thinking? She hadn't been.

Typing an apology text when three sharp knocks rattled her front door.

Her heart slammed against her ribs. **Donovan**. Her fingers shook as she swiped to her security app, and the camera revealed Damien standing under her porch light, his face a map of bruises and cuts.

She yanked the door open, words dying in her throat. Blood stained his shirt, and his knuckles were split raw. Before she could step toward him, his hands framed her face, callused thumbs brushing her cheekbones as his eyes searched hers with an intensity that made her knees weak.

"Are you all right?" His voice was gravel and whiskey, and something deep in her belly clenched at the genuine concern radiating from him.

"Come inside." She stepped back, giving him room, then locked the deadbolt again. "The question is, are you all right? You look like you got hit by a truck."

Purple bruising bloomed along his jawline. Without thinking, she reached up to trace it gently. "Who did this to you?"

His eyes—God, they were so blue—never left her face. "I'm fine. Tell me what happened."

"I may have overreacted, but I'm not sure. I needed to talk to someone and..." Her hand dropped from his face, hovering over his chest where something dark stained the fabric. "How about you shower first? I'll make us something to eat, and then we can figure this out. You look worse off than I am right now."

---

Steam billowed from the bathroom as Damien let hot water wash away blood and adrenaline. He was certain Sadie's text had to do with Donovan. And whatever it was, it frightened her enough to reach out to him.

—-

Sadie busied herself in the kitchen, trying not to think about him naked just twenty feet away, water cascading over what she'd glimpsed of his broad shoulders and muscled chest.

**Focus**. She stared blindly into her refrigerator, finally grabbing leftover pasta salad and some sausage to dice up. The focaccia bread she'd bought yesterday would round out the simple meal. Not fancy, but it would do.

The shower shut off, and she heard the soft thud of his footsteps on her bathroom tiles. Every sound seemed amplified, or at least it did to her. When he appeared in her kitchen doorway wearing nothing but one of her bath towels slung low around his hips, her brain short-circuited.

Water droplets clung to the defined muscles of his chest and arms. His dark hair was slicked back, emphasizing the sharp angles of his face. The bruises looked worse now, purple-black against his skin, but they didn't diminish the raw masculinity that filled her small kitchen.

He moved closer, and she caught the scent of her jasmine body wash on his skin. One hand lifted to tuck a strand of hair behind her ear, his touch gentle despite the power she could sense coiled beneath his surface.

"Do I make you nervous, lu me tesoro?" The words rolled off his tongue like silk, foreign and intimate.

"What does that mean?" Her voice came out breathier than intended.

He took the one last step that closed the space between them, his fingers trailing up her arm and leaving fire in their wake. "It means...my treasure."

Before she could process that endearment, his mouth was on hers. The kiss started soft, questioning, then deepened as she melted against him. His tongue swept across her lower lip, and she opened for him with a sound that was part sigh, part surrender.

—

She was the sweetest, most delicious thing he'd ever tasted. A growl low, starting in his belly, then erupting from his lips as his beast stirred to the female in his arms.

Heat radiated from his body as his hands found the hem of her shirt. He paused, giving her time to object. He knew this might seem fast, but he couldn't stop himself. Cool air hit her skin, making her shiver, and his eyes darkened as they roamed over her.

"You're beautiful," he murmured, his lips finding the sensitive spot below her ear.

…

She'd never let anyone touch her like this. Her gift made physical contact dangerous—too many unwanted visions, too many invasive memories. But with Damien, there was only sensation, the slide of his mouth against her throat and the way her body came alive under his hands.

…

Moans wrapped around them. Damien's thoughts turned to Donovan and the threat he posed. A surge of power coursed through him, fueling his need for her. With deliberate intent, his actions took on a primal edge, his fangs punching through his gums and filling his mouth, and he bit into her golden skin, just where neck met shoulder, injecting his venom as a symbol of possession and devotion that transcended mere physicality.

He was in euphoria. A high like nothing he'd ever felt. Dominance surging through every cell of his body. This was fate at play.

Then slowly it surfaced. Etched into her skin by a blend of supernatural and ancient magic, his mating mark appeared. Though Sadie would remain unaware for several days, it was unmistakably visible to other males, exuding a scent that would not go unnoticed.

......

His lips traced a path to her shoulder, tongue swirling against her skin. She tilted her head, giving him better access, lost in the building heat between them. This was how it felt to want someone, to crave their touch more than your next breath.

Her arousal flared. If this was how he began, she couldn't imagine surviving him until they reached the ending. But she wanted to.

Sadie had never had sex. She rarely touched others, her gift not allowing for that. But now, here with Damien, she wanted everything.

Then a sharp pain blazed through her shoulder. Not a gentle nip or playful bite, but teeth sinking deep into her flesh. She gasped, shock and betrayal flooding through her as she realized what he'd done.

"Stop!" She shoved against his chest, stumbling backwards. "What the hell, Damien?"

The taste of copper filled her mouth where she'd bitten her own tongue in surprise. Her shoulder throbbed, and she pressed her hand against it, feeling wetness she didn't want to identify.

"Sadie, I was lost in the moment." His eyes had changed—the pupils more elongated.. "You're intoxicating. I can hardly think around you."

"You had no right!" Anger overrode the desire that had been clouding her judgment. "I trusted you, and you—what kind of sick game is this?"

"It's not a game—"

"Get out." The words tore from her throat. "Just get out."

Pain flashed across his features, followed by something darker. For a moment, she thought he might argue, might refuse to leave. Then he stepped back, his jaw clenched.

"Fine." The single word was clipped, cold.

She blinked, and he was gone. Not walked away—gone. Vanished like smoke, leaving only the lingering scent of jasmine and the ache in her shoulder.

Sadie sank onto her couch, pressing the heels of her hands against her eyes. First Donovan, now Damien. Maybe Father Sullivan had been right all those years ago—maybe she really was cursed.

---

Damien materialized in his own living room, power crackling around him like static electricity. Books tumbled from shelves as his control shattered, and he swept his arm across the coffee table, sending everything crashing to the floor.

"She belongs to me," he snarled to the empty room. "The mark proves it, whether she understands or not."

But even as fury consumed him, a small voice whispered that he'd made a terrible mistake. She was human. She didn't know what the bite meant, what he'd just claimed. He'd taken her choice away in the most primal way possible.

The realization only fed his rage, because now he had to live with what he'd done—and what he'd lost.

# Chapter 13

Damien's fists trembled at his sides, knuckles white as bone. The mirror across the room reflected a stranger—eyes wild, jaw clenched so tight his teeth might crack. He had lost control, something that hadn't happened in decades. Yet when he'd learned about Sadie's boss, when he'd seen the shadow of fear in her eyes as she spoke about the man, something primal had awakened in him. The need to protect her had consumed every rational thought.

His fingers traced the air where her shoulder had been, remembering the moment his fangs had pierced her skin. Only one woman before had ever borne his mark—a mark that had remained dull and lifeless, never taking on his color or scent. His best friend had warned him then: "She's not your soulmate, Dame." But love had made him deaf to wisdom, and the price had been a life shrouded in darkness, guilt gnawing at his soul like acid.

A smile tugged at the corner of his mouth despite the storm raging inside him. The mark on Sadie's shoulder pulsed with life—green iridescence that caught the light like emerald fire. His family crest coiled around her shoulder blade and traced down her spine, undeniable proof that she belonged to him as surely as he belonged to her.

The thought of Donovan's hands on her made his vision blur red. How could someone so pure be tangled up with that piece of filth? Everyone in their circles knew what Donovan was—a man who'd sell his own mother's soul if the price was right, and Sadie probably had no idea what kind of monster employed her.

The change hit him like lightning splitting a tree. His human form dissolved as Typhon emerged, serpents writhing from his shoulders, hissing their fury. Furniture exploded around him— the oak desk splintering, books scattered like fallen leaves, the leather chair reduced to shreds.

The door burst open. Bane's boots crunched over broken glass as he surveyed the wreckage, his weathered face pale beneath his red beard.

"Damien, laddie, what in hell's name—" Bane's voice cut through the chaos, steady despite the destruction surrounding them.

Damien's serpents retracted as he forced himself back into human form, chest heaving. "Bane, I..." His voice cracked like a teenager's. "I did something I never fucking thought I would do. I lost control and I bit her. I bit Sadie and gave her my mark."

Bane's eyebrows shot up to his hairline. "Ye what now? Damien, that's not like ye at all, lad."

"I couldn't stop myself." Damien's hands shook as he ran them through his hair. "This rage just took over, and I—"

"Have ye lost yer bloody mind?" Bane stepped closer, glass crunching under his boots. The concern etched in the lines around his eyes aged him a decade.

"I did it to protect her from Donovan." The words tore from Damien's throat raw and desperate.

Bane dragged a calloused hand down his face, his shoulders sagging. He'd seen Damien infatuated before, but this was different. This was the kind of obsession that destroyed men. "Maybe ye should slow down just a wee bit, aye?"

Damien's fist connected with the wall, plaster crumbling around his knuckles. Blood welled up, but he felt nothing except the fire in his chest. **"She's mine, Bane!** The mark proves it—she's my mate!"

"Aye, I can see that." Bane's voice gentled, the way it did when he was trying to calm a spooked horse. "But does the lass know what ye are? Can she handle being mated to the god of monsters? Yer venom alone could kill her if she's not ready for it. There's a reason the rest of us chose our own kind, Dame."

The serpents stirred beneath Damien's skin, ready to strike. "She's my mate. End of fucking story."

Bane's hand landed heavy on Damien's shoulder, grip firm enough to anchor him. "Aye, I ken that weel enough, but she's only human, ye see. Our world would fair terrify the lass—all the darkness an' the violence, ken.". I don't want ye to scare her so badly she runs from ye. That would destroy ye, and we both know it."

The fight drained out of Damien like air from a punctured tire. His shoulders slumped as Bane's words hit home. Another loss would kill him—he'd barely survived the last one. The image of Sadie looking at him with fear instead of the warmth he'd seen earlier made his chest tighten until he could barely breathe.

But then he pictured her standing beside him, chin raised, unafraid of the darkness that had swallowed so much of his life. She had to understand that everything he'd done came from love, even if his methods were unforgivable. The battle ahead would test them both, but the mark binding them together was stronger than fear.

It had to be.

# Chapter 14

She groaned in her dreams—a sensual slide of his lips over hers, stirring her awake. Then the scene shifted: whimpers replaced euphoria, grief shadowed everything, and her erotic dream twisted into a nightmare.

She'd given herself freely to Damien. Stepping into his arms had felt like coming home. When had she ever done that with anyone? Never. And then he'd deliberately hurt her.

Her overactive mind kept her tossing between sleep and wakefulness all night, the ache in her shoulder forgotten amid the chaos of thoughts.

Last night, she'd dabbed antiseptic on the two rows of bite marks, her fingers drifting to the tender skin while she tried to find sleep. But sleep refused to come.

He'd let her down. His betrayal finally forced her to stare into the darkness of her room. Anger burned hotter—at herself, for thinking he was someone he wasn't, for opening the door and letting her hopes of him inside.

"Stupid Sadie," she whispered into the empty room. Another stupid mistake. At least now she saw it for what it was. She didn't need another Donovan, and she definitely didn't need to add to the shit pile she already carried.

She wished she had a best friend like others did. But she'd always kept people at arm's length, even as a kid. Since hooking up with Donovan, that distance had widened—he was always watching, and she didn't want to put anyone else in his line of sight.

Maybe she'd see if Maya wanted to meet for coffee. It had been at least a month since they'd last seen each other. Maya always made her feel lighter, always giving of herself, even if Sadie never returned the favor.

She pushed out of bed, her hand brushing her phone. The glowing display read 5:32 a.m. Three hours of sleep would have to do today. Her bare feet found the soft carpet, and she flicked the bathroom light switch. The harsh fluorescent flickered on, stabbing her retinas.

Sadie gathered her hair to one side and tugged down the strap of her cami, her eyes fixed on the fading bite marks.

They were almost gone, which was strange, yet they still throbbed—halfway between a bad itch and a dull ache.

She needed a shower. Her chestnut eyes drifted to the spot where Damien had stood, washing away everything he'd been covered in. He'd never told her where he'd been or what had happened to get him covered in blood.

She shook her head. It didn't matter anymore. He could do whatever he wanted with whoever he wanted.

Deciding to erase every trace of his presence, she grabbed the bottle of Scrubbing Bubbles from under the sink and sprayed the entire stall from top to bottom, letting it sit for the full fifteen minutes, just as the directions instructed.

She sank onto the toilet lid, checking the time—5:37 a.m.—then crossed her legs and arms with renewed resolve. She'd figure out her mess herself. She'd keep telling herself that for the next fourteen minutes while the timer counted down, then wash away whatever was left of him. She wouldn't reach out to Damien again. Screw him.

---

By the time lunch rolled around, exhaustion pressed down on her shoulders. She felt like she'd already put in a full day—the sleep deprivation running her on empty. It didn't help that she hadn't eaten last night, only managing a cup of black coffee this morning—no sugar, no cream, nothing to soften the bitter edge that matched her mood.

Thoughts of Damien kept surfacing like unwanted bubbles. She shoved them down, replacing them with the data she was supposed to analyze. Brain fog clung to her today, but dammit, she refused to indulge in the whole woe-is-me drama. She was strong. She'd get through this, just like she had everything else.

"Sadie? I don't mean to pry, but you haven't moved in like twenty minutes."

So absorbed in her own world, she hadn't heard Roger enter their work area—the space where their desks and computers were set up.

"Just thinking, I suppose. You know me—I get wrapped up, and it's like I've dropped off somewhere else." Her words weren't far from the truth. "But maybe it's time for a lunch break."

She pushed her chair back, grabbed her bag from the bottom drawer. Maybe some sunshine and fresh air would help. "I'll be back in an hour. It's quiet now—maybe you should take yours too."

And not waiting for him to possibly ask to come along, she headed out into the main part of the museum.

Her heels clicked against the tile floor, steady in her mind as she sidestepped visitors milling around the exhibits. It was busier than usual—then she remembered: Seniors Day. Every second Wednesday was a big hit, considering how often she'd had to duck out of someone's way.

That was good, though. Modern tech might steal some of the magic, but seeing history up close still made her feel alive. Whether it was ingrained because of her psychometry, she wasn't sure. But when her visions weren't terrifying, it was like having front-row seats to the past.

"Sadie." Donovan's voice snapped her from her wandering thoughts, just like Roger's had. "Are you heading out for lunch? It's about that time. Care for some company?"

She hoped her face didn't betray how awful his question sounded. She just wanted to be alone.

"I was actually going to run a few errands and grab something quick." The lie sounded convincing—even to herself.

He lifted her chin with one fingertip, his gaze locking her in place. "That's not good, ma petite. You've lost weight, and you look pale. I'm feeding you, so no excuses. Come." His hand found her elbow, guiding her toward the bank of elevators leading to the underground parking lot.

This was not what she wanted. She just wanted it to be a D-free day; no Donovan, no Damien.

The elevator door swooshed open. A couple exited. Donovan steered her inside, hitting the close button before stepping closer, forcing her into the corner of the six-by-six cell—that's what it felt like.

"Now tell me what's made you upset today. Don't say nothing." His voice was low but firm. "I saw you on the internal cameras while you worked, and you're not yourself."

He was too close. She couldn't breathe. After last night, her anxiety was at a breaking point.

"Donovan, step back." Her voice was steadier than she felt.

"Sadie, watch yourself. I'm here because I care. You could show a little gratitude."

"I was fine going to lunch alone. You're the one who didn't give me a choice." The words burst out before she could stop them, leaving both of them stunned into silence.

Anger tightened his jaw, and she knew she'd messed up badly. His hand shot up, grabbing her roughly around the back of her neck, scraping where Damien had bitten her.

A cry of pain escaped her lips. She jerked away, her own hand instinctively pressing against the tender spot.

"What's wrong? Are you hurt?"

She slipped past him, eyes flicking upward, just waiting for the L to illuminate for the lower level.

"It's nothing."

And she hadn't seen it coming. She hadn't felt him move. One hand swiping her hair out of the way, the other pulling her blouse off her shoulder.

Silence.

Utter silence.

Then a trickle of fear seeped into every cell of her body as a tone she'd never heard from him before filled the space.

"What the fuck is this, Sadie?" His tone was dangerous and threatening.

She shrugged as the overhead ping sounded, the door swooshing open. She didn't look his way. As she went to step out, he grabbed her, pinning her against the wall.

"You let that filth Damien mark you? Are you stupid? You let him rut between your legs when you've given me no time of day? After everything I've done for you? I could kill you right now."

Their faces were inches apart. She saw it then—something dark, something malevolent flickering in his eyes.

"What do you mean he marked me?" Her voice trembled. "And how do you know it was Damien?"

A twisted laugh rose from his throat, like a scream in a horror movie. "Oh, Sadie girl. You messed up. But here's the thing: I'm not letting him have you. **You're mine!"**

She didn't know where her strength came from, but she shoved him back and sprinted out the open door just as a few others moved in. She didn't look back, just kept heading toward the ramp leading out to the street. Her head pounded from fear, and unease curled tightly in her stomach.

What had Damien done?

<h1 style="text-align:center">Chapter 15</h1>

He was wound tight, ready to uncoil at the first idiot to step out of line. It would only take the slightest provocation, and he'd take a life.

The hard thrum of his V-twin vibrated between his thighs and up his spine. The muscles through his arms and shoulders rippled with tension as he focused on the darkening road stretching before him.

The warm night air caressed Donovan's skin—no jacket, no helmet. He didn't give a shit about human law. The only law he lived by was his own. He'd scraped and bled his way to his position of power, clawing up from nothing as a child—a bastard son of a whore. A low-bred demon so far down the food chain he'd been used as a boot swipe.

But he'd watched and learned, then watched some more. He'd studied all the ins and outs of anything that would make him money, taking jobs no one else wanted on both sides of the wall—human and supernatural.

Then one day at the tracks, he'd bet everything he had on a longshot: Burnt Bones, a discolored thoroughbred on her way to the slaughterhouse in the very near future. When that horse paid out at 50-1, he'd grabbed his cash and headed for the front gates, planning his first stop at a men's department store he'd never been able to afford. For years, he'd only stolen glimpses at the high-end suits as he walked past the window every other day.

But that thought got waylaid when two goons blindsided him barely twenty paces outside Santa Anita Park and shoved him into a Lincoln.

"How did you know that horse would come in today? He's never placed, shown, or nothing. How did you know?"

Donovan knew who confronted him, knew exactly who he was facing. Everyone knew who Luca Castille was—the right-hand man for Frank Costi. And Mr. Costi was the man who ran all the illegal activity along the western coastline. You either did things his way or you disappeared. He was everything Donovan hoped to be.

"I know people who know people, and I listen. I got lucky today."

What Donovan didn't tell them was that he'd paid off a lore demon in his favorite street candy to possess the horse and give it the legs it needed to win the mile run. Donovan would have done it himself, but possession wasn't one of the traits gifted to him by either parent. Whether the thoroughbred died afterwards was of no consequence to him. He just needed the payout—he had plans.

He kept his answer to the other male simple. He'd learned that overconfidence could fuck everything up, learned that lesson the hard way.

Luca settled further into the plush backing of his seat, a trail of cigarette smoke playing between them. "You know who I am? Who I represent?"

"I do, Mr. Castille."

"These people you know—do I already know them? And if I don't, maybe I should." His hand lifted to his mouth, taking a drag. Donovan wished he had one, too. "I lost today, which I don't like. You'll come with me and we can talk."

Donovan knew there was no choice, and he'd be stupid to backtalk. The Costi family had their hands in everything. The one advantage he had was that he wasn't human. So for now, he'd take this moment for what it was—stay quiet and watch.

"I don't mind talking, Mr. Castille." With that, he leaned back, taking note of which direction they were traveling. Maybe his luck was about to change. Maybe he could worm his way in—he was good at that.

---

He shot a quick glance at the road as a semi decided that passing a biker on a curve was a smart fucking thing to do. Donovan let them because he was too far down memory lane to give a shit right now. On any other day, he'd play chicken with the driver and weave back and forth in front of them, egging them on.

But today, that mark on Sadie's shoulder had struck a nerve. He knew a mating mark when he saw one, and he knew that serpentine snake represented Damien—he'd seen similar images on the man's letterhead.

He'd always had someone keeping an eye on her. Not every second of every day, but she was his investment. She made him a shit ton of money, and he expected that to continue.

As far as he knew, she'd only met Damien the one time he'd sent her to deliver the shabtis. How the bloody hell had this shit show happened?

His problem now was Damien Nikolas. The male wasn't going to let Sadie go now that she wore his brand. And even though Donovan himself was a force to reckon with, considering everything he'd heard about the head of the Sicilian mafia, it wouldn't be smart to start a war he wasn't sure he could win.

Tiny flickers of LA appeared far off in the distance—pinpricks of life in the darkness he'd just ridden through. Sadie was now off-limits by demon law. Fortunately for him, rules had never applied. Nobody took what was his. Nobody. The question was: would Sadie accept it? She didn't even know she'd been marked, so maybe Damien wasn't being forthright with her. Maybe this was where he could drive a wedge.

He pulled the throttle, and a smile no one would see crossed his face. A ride always cleared his head. It would be his pleasure to tutor Sadie on the world of the demonic. He'd kept that part of himself tightly controlled around her, though to this day, he wasn't sure why. Maybe because she was business, and he didn't want to cross those lines with her. Her emotions were so often on high alert because of her gift, and he needed her focused to keep that gold mine working.

She'd never shown interest in anyone, including himself. He'd assumed she was so scarred from her childhood that she simply preferred to stay on her own.

Not much surprised him, but this had. His smile twisted into a leer. Let Damien watch as he slowly and methodically took his mate from him.

# Chapter 16

The unease that had been swirling in her gut plunged deeper, like a block of concrete settling in her stomach. Donovan's liquid gaze seemed to follow her even though she'd left him in that elevator. Heat prickled across her back as she hurried down the sidewalk away from the museum, his presence chasing her like a shadow.

She abandoned her car in its reserved spot. Papers and journals remained scattered across her desk. Donovan would have to make excuses to her co-workers when she didn't return from lunch.

This wasn't over—just the beginning of turmoil between Donovan and Damien, with her caught in the crossfire.

The old urge clawed at her chest: find a corner, a small hole in a back alley like when she was younger, burrow deep underneath her hoodie, and pretend the world didn't exist. Just the armor of solitude that no one could breach.

Shivers racked her body as she walked, her heart hammering against her ribs. Every footstep behind her could be one of Donovan's men coming to drag her back.

Her lungs burned despite the steady rhythm of her breathing.

Now what? Where could she go? What options did she have left?

A taxi rounded the corner at the upcoming intersection. She waved frantically, and the window lowered to reveal a middle-aged gentleman behind the wheel, dressed like an old-world scholar.

"Are you available?" Desperation crept into Sadie's voice despite her efforts to sound calm.

"I am, Miss. Hop in. Where will I be taking you?"

His accent carried traces of British roots, softened by years in the States. Where did she want to go? She needed time to think, space to breathe.

Sadie slid into the backseat and pulled the door shut. Her eyes swept the sidewalk where she'd been walking, then met the driver's gentle gaze in the rearview mirror as he waited for her answer.

Her mind and heart latched onto the old boardwalk at Santa Monica Pier. Memories surfaced of nights spent safe among the rocks and boulders across the highway from the famous landmark, days walking miles of oceanfront, eyes sharp for anything that could earn her money.

"Santa Monica Pier, please."

"You sure, Miss? That's quite a drive and not inexpensive." The care in his question nearly brought tears to her eyes.

"I'm sure. Thank you."

His protective nod warmed something inside her chest. As he checked each mirror and glanced over his shoulder, Sadie opened her bag and found her earbuds. She left them disconnected, letting the ends rest in her purse—she wasn't in the mood to talk. He seemed like a sweetheart, but conversation felt impossible. City scenes blurred past the window in one continuous reel while her thoughts tangled around the men in her life, all for the wrong reasons.

---

These miles of sand and water had been her confidante. She'd spilled fears and dreams to the crashing waves and wind that whipped her hair into chaos.

She hadn't returned here since Donovan altered her life, mostly her own fault. She could have turned her steering wheel in this direction anytime.

Maybe the clarity that always came when she walked these stretches of sand would force her to face her own concerns and anxieties.

Her gaze drifted left across the busy freeway, vehicles rushing toward unknown destinations. Among the dry grasses, she searched for that familiar cluster of rocks where she'd curled herself into a pretzel—mostly alone, sometimes with Katie tagging along. The ocean's rhythm had been her lullaby until seagulls interrupted at dawn's crack, refusing to be ignored. Then she'd head down to spend her few dollars on a breakfast burrito and coffee. Usually alone—Katie occasionally joining her—but solitude felt safest.

Katie had been nice, another teenage runaway who loved to talk nonstop. Sadie preferred quiet. When Katie announced she was going wandering and would see her around, Sadie would tell her to be safe and leave it at that. That was the way of being homeless.

Time was running out before Damien or Donovan found her trail. She didn't know how they'd track her, but she wouldn't put anything past either of them.

Neither man belonged to this world. She didn't understand what that meant, but what she did know was that she could be killed, and she wouldn't put murder past Donovan now, not after witnessing the rage that had transformed him in the elevator.

She rarely saw him lose control, but in that moment, a side of him emerged that planted the fear of everything unholy deep in her bones.

She'd buried her head in the sand regarding him and his world—ironic as her sandals dangled from her fingertips while warm sand shifted between her toes. She'd allowed herself to be led in so many ways.

Outsiders would assume she lived the perfect life, never knowing she carried chains every day, binding herself to Donovan. And now Damien had marked her as well.

She lifted her phone from her pocket, fingers hovering before typing: *a mark from being bitten.* Emotions crashed over her as she scrolled through every link, locking onto one bold text: a mark or brand on a person's body, signifying their permanent bond to another, typically the result of a bite.

Also known as a claiming bite or mating mark.

Seagull caws faded. Ocean waves fell silent. A cocoon wrapped around her like she'd been thrust into a private vision. The mark on her shoulder flared to life, heat confirming what she'd just read, reminding her exactly who had bitten her.

"No."

The word whispered first, then grew into a full sentence, a declaration. She wouldn't be anyone's property anymore.

Sand burned against her feet as she turned and pushed toward the street. The taxi queue stretched short at this time of day.

She'd go home, even though that was risky, pack a bag and disappear, at least temporarily. She could survive with a knapsack; she'd done it for years. She'd been smart, stashing away enough cash to avoid credit cards. No trail to follow, she hoped.

Time—that's all she needed. Time to figure out how to break free from Donovan and decide how to eliminate this ache in her shoulder.

Didn't peroxide fix almost anything?

# Chapter 17

Another day had passed, and Damien's hands still trembled when he thought about what he'd done. He stared at his reflection in the bathroom mirror, running his fingers through his hair. The bite mark he'd left on Sadie's shoulder burned in his memory. She was like the most intoxicating whiskey, and she demanded a slow savouring.

Her laugh held warmth and depth, her words sweet yet sharpened with wit that could cut through his defenses. Each conversation revealed another layer, another secret.

Damien pressed his palms against the marble countertop. Never before had he lost control like that. His fangs had descended without permission, piercing her skin before he could stop himself. But the serpentine mark now coiled around her shoulder confirmed what his soul already knew—she was his mate. Nothing would change that future. Not even the resistance of the stunning blonde who had stolen his heart and refused to give it back.

Damien grabbed his phone and dialed. Enzo's raspy voice answered on the third ring. "What's up, boss man?"

Damien's laugh came out strained. "Did I wake you, old man?"

"Nah, I just had my soul sucked out of me. My wife is a beast when it comes to—"

"TMI, Enzo." Damien cut him off, pacing across his bedroom. "I need a favor. Get yourself up and ready. I need you to keep an eye on Sadie."

"Trouble in paradise?" Enzo's voice carried that familiar teasing lilt.

"Shut up, vamp, and get your ass moving. I marked Sadie. She's my true mate." The words came out harsher than intended.

Enzo coughed, and Damien could picture him sitting up in bed. "You did what, Dame? Is this a joke?"

Damien's jaw clenched. "It's not a joke. I expect your report within the hour."

He ended the call and threw the phone onto his bed. His throat burned with thirst—not for blood, but for something stronger. Closing his eyes, he teleported to Enigma, materializing behind the bar where Bane stood, counting inventory bottles.

Without a word to his oldest friend, Damien reached for the absinthe. The first shot burned down his throat like liquid fire. Then another. By the sixth, Bane's massive hand closed around the bottle, lifting it out of reach.

Damien's eyebrow arched as he watched the hellhound return the bottle to its shelf. "I wasn't done with that."

Bane scrubbed his hand down his weathered face, his Scottish accent thicker when he was concerned. "Damien, ye are my best mate. We've kenned each other since we were wee bairns. So what I'm about tae say might piss ye off, but ye need tae hear it." He leaned against the bar, his brown eyes serious. "Dame, what ye did is nae okay. She's but a mere human, an' you are a god. Ye do ken yer venom could have killed the lassie, aye?"

Damien's muscles coiled tight. The old hellhound spoke the truth, but admitting it felt like swallowing glass. "She is my mate, Bane. It isn't like it was before." His voice dropped to a growl. "You know that bitch I married didn't even take my mark. I should have walked away from her, but I didn't, and I paid the ultimate price. This is fucking different, hound. My mark glows like a beacon on Sadie's flesh. She is mine. End of story."

Bane stepped around the bar, his heavy boots echoing in the empty club. He placed a calloused hand on Damien's shoulder. "Dame, then away wi' ye and go tae her. Apologize. Tell the lassie who ye really are, an' mind ye dinnae lose yer cool." His grip tightened. "Enzo called right before ye got here. Sadie just got home. Now away an' show her how a mate is supposed tae be, aye?"

---

The evening air bit at Damien's skin as he stood on Sadie's doorstep. His knuckles rapped against the wood—quick, hard knocks that echoed his racing heartbeat. The weight of his mistake pressed down on his shoulders like stone. Through the crack beneath her door, he caught the faint whiff of vanilla and something else. Something that made his jaw clench.

Another male scent-a demon scent.

When Sadie finally opened the door, her blue eyes held a storm of hurt and defiance. The soft lamplight from inside painted gold highlights in her blonde hair and cast shadows beneath her eyes. Without thinking, Damien reached out to brush a strand behind her ear, his fingers lingering against her skin.

"I know I was a complete ass, and I am sorry. I just got lost in you, in us." His voice cracked despite his efforts to sound controlled.

Sadie's silence cut deeper than any words could have. Her arms crossed over her chest, a barrier between them. Damien felt the snowball of emotions building in his chest—guilt, regret, possessiveness, need. He'd fucked up badly, and they both knew it.

When she turned away, dismissing him, her movement carried uncertainty. The scent of another man clung to her clothes like smoke, bitter and wrong. Damien's vision sharpened, his breathing deepened. With deliberate steps, he closed the gap between them, his hand catching her shoulder and turning her back to face him.

His inner demons whispered. His urges won.

Their lips crashed together in a kiss fueled by desperation and longing. Heat swept through both of them, igniting the spark that had been smoldering since their first meeting. Sadie might not want to want him, but her body betrayed her— melting against his, her hands fisting in his shirt.

With tenderness that surprised them both, Damien lifted her off her feet. Her legs wrapped instinctively around his waist as they lost themselves in tongues and breathless moans. Each touch spoke of unspoken desire and a connection that transcended rational thought.

He navigated the familiar hallway to her bedroom by memory, his lips never leaving hers. Only when he reached her bed did he break the kiss, tossing her onto the mattress with controlled force. Hunger gnawed at his insides—primal, demanding. He tried to remember to be gentle, but control slipped through his fingers like sand.

The taste of her blood still lingered on his tongue from their first encounter. Pure. Untouched. Virgin. The knowledge that he would be her first and only sent possessive fire through his veins.

Damien's hands found the button of her jeans, pulling them down to her ankles. A low growl rumbled from his throat when he saw the black lace panties underneath—his favorite color. A small patch of blonde hair peeked through the delicate fabric, making his cock strain painfully against his pants.

He pushed her knees apart, making room for himself between her thighs. Restraint abandoned him. Dropping to his knees beside the bed, his gaze fixated on that wisp of lace. His tongue swiped across her center, the friction of fabric and flesh making her arch beneath him.

Her hands flew to his shoulders, blunt nails digging crescents into his skin. His name fell from her lips—long, drawn-out, desperate. Music to his ears.

She was panting, begging him not to stop when he'd barely begun. He nibbled her clit through the lace, her body jerking in response. Her whimpers had to be the sexiest sound he'd ever heard.

He sucked harder. His name became an anguished scream as her orgasm crashed over her, her sweet nectar coating his tongue. His mate tasted like pure sin, his demon snarling in his head to tear away what remained of her clothes and feast.

Damien struggled against the urge to devour her completely. His cock throbbed, demanding attention. He stood and undressed with jerky, impatient movements—his erection hard as granite, pearls of precum glistening at the tip.

Using his powers, he made Sadie's remaining clothes vanish, joining his on the floor. She was too lost in the waves of ecstasy to notice the impossibility.

She was fucking beautiful. Her breasts were full with rose-tipped nipples that would fit perfectly in his palms. His gaze traveled lower, taking in the defined muscles of her abdomen, the suntan lines riding high on her hips. The wetness glistening in her blonde curls, her folds bare and pink, her scent setting up a growl deep in his chest.

Perfection. And he couldn't wait another second.

He climbed onto the bed, hovering over her trembling form. His lips found hers again, his tongue sharing the taste of her release. His cock nudged against her entrance, pressing in slightly. Sadie pulled back from their kiss, a raspy plea falling from her lips.

His head dipped to her breasts. He bit her nipple as his cock slowly entered her core, her inner muscles desperately trying to accommodate his size. He pumped slowly, in and out, fighting the sweet torture of her tightness. Holy fuck, she was so tight he wasn't sure how long he could last.

Her legs lifted, wrapping around his waist. Her hips arched to meet his thrust, and he broke through her barrier.

She moaned his name, clamping down on his cock like a vice. He rocked back, then slammed deep into her again. The wet sounds of their joining drove him toward the point of no return. They were both lost in a sex-drunk haze, his grunts mixing with her cries, sweat beading on his chest and back.

He pulled out and flipped her over, his arm sliding beneath her to pull her up on her knees. Without waiting for her to steady herself, he plowed into her drenched pussy to the hilt, then pulled back until only his tip remained inside her. His lust-filled gaze drank in the sight of his serpent mark imprinted down her spine, and he thrust again, making her buck wildly.

Damien quickened his pace, his balls tightening with impending release. Sadie's whimpers and pleas were music to his ears. He felt the first violent ripple race across his cock, and then she screamed—a sound part feral, part ecstasy that he'd remember forever.

He followed her over the edge. Her name roared from his lips as his seed filled her womb, their bodies completely lost to everything but each other.

As the sharp edge of climax released them, Damien collapsed on the bed, still buried inside her. He pulled her against his chest, both of them fighting to catch their breath.

"You are perfection, Peach," he whispered against her ear, his voice husky with satisfaction. "And you're mine. I want you to pack up your favorite things. You are going home with me, where you belong. You are my mate, the other half of my soul."

Sadie stilled, then shifted. Their bodies parted as she tried to pull away, but his arm tightened, unwilling to release her. She wasn't having it. Rolling over to face him, her eyebrows pinched together in confusion.

"I am not going to move in with you. This is my home, Damien. Surely you understand."

Rage flared hot in his chest. What the hell was wrong with her? He slid out of bed, snatching his clothes and pulling them on with sharp, angry movements. He kept his hands busy—if he didn't, he'd grab her, and he didn't trust himself at that moment.

Didn't she understand she was his? He wanted her with him where he could keep her safe and protected. They were mated—didn't that mean something to her? His anger reached a critical level, pressure building behind his eyes.

"Get dressed, Peach. We're going home. I won't take no for an answer." His glare changed—he could feel it. Typhon pressed against the edges of his control.

Sadie pushed herself out of bed and walked over to him, poking him in the chest with her finger. "I have no idea what you think should happen, but it's not happening. Mated? What does that even mean? I am staying here, Damien, whether you like it or not."

Damien took a step back, his monster seething inside. He tried to wrangle Typhon back, but there was no stopping him now. The transformation ripped through him, and her bedroom exploded around them—furniture splintering, glass shattering, walls cracking.

Sadie screamed and tried to run. Typhon's massive hand closed around her waist, bringing her close to his scaled face.

His voice came out as a deep rumble, split between human speech and monster growls. "It seems Damien forgot to tell you who he is. So let me tell you precisely what we are." His grip tightened possessively. "Damien is the god of monsters. I am his monster form. He is the son of Gaia, goddess of earth, and Tartarus, primordial god of the abyss. He didn't want to introduce us this way, but you gave him no choice. Like he said, we aren't taking no for an answer."

He held Sadie close to his chest to stop her trembling, clothes reappearing on her frame as he teleported them both to the hellhound's home. Bane and Kimora looked up in shock from where they sat on their couch. They immediately bowed their heads as Typhon shifted back into Damien.

Sadie pulled away from him and ran to Kimora, partially hiding behind the smaller woman.

"Sadie is going to stay with you two for a bit until she gets used to the fact that we are mated. Then she will move in with me." Damien's voice brooked no argument.

Bane ran his hand through his hair in obvious frustration. "I reckon our wee talk didnae go as planned, eh?"

Damien shook his head as Kimora interrupted, her voice sharp with disapproval. "Do you think it was a good idea to turn into Typhon and scare the living shit out of Sadie? Are you certain she is your mate? You did think your ex was as well."

"You watch your fucking tone with me, Kimora." Damien's eyes flashed dangerously. "Look at her fucking shoulder and see for yourself."

Kimora turned to face Sadie and gently spun her around. She slid Sadie's shirt off her shoulder and gasped. The serpent mark ran from her shoulder down the middle of her spine, its green hue shimmering in the lamplight. Kimora leaned close and whispered against Sadie's ear, "We still have another card to play."

"Damien," Kimora said aloud, "she might wear your mark but until you consummate your mating, the mark doesn't mean shit."

"Kimora, be gentle wi' yer words, my love. Damien is hurtin an' so is wee Sadie. Mind that he's our king, aye?" Bane's voice carried gentle reproach.

A smirk tugged at the corners of Damien's lips. "We just fucked."

Kimora's mouth fell open. Damien had found his true mate. No wonder he was acting so irrational. She touched Sadie's arm gently, her tone matching. "Looks like you've been fucked twice tonight, Sadie."

Damien's gaze locked on Sadie, never wavering. "Indeed, she has. I will be back for my mate. I'll give her time to think things through." He knew he was being an utter and complete asshole, but he didn't care at this moment. She was his. He'd kill anyone who got in his way. He'd found his one, and so had his monster.

# Chapter 18

She'd chanced fate and had the taxi driver take her straight into the underground garage, stopping right behind where her car sat waiting. Three minutes—that's all it took—and she was in and on her way to her apartment. Anxiety cranked to maximum as she kept checking her rearview mirror. If luck was on her side, which she felt she was due some of, she'd need maybe a half hour to stuff a bag and be back on the road to who the hell knew where.

This might not be the mature way to handle this, but both men together were suffocating. She felt like she was being crammed into a cage.

The knock came first. The swipe of her screen second. Damien's face on her security app third. No point in ignoring him—he could get in as easily as Donovan.

She'd tried to steel herself, add some metal to her backbone. That was the plan until she opened the door, and there he was. God, he was beautiful, and his scent went straight into her pores. But with it came deep disappointment because she had been feeling a certain way about him, letting him in slowly around the walls she hid behind. Maybe her daydreams were more fairytale, and that was her fault.

His apology made her anger rise and mix with her hurt—an unsteady cocktail. She stepped back, knowing he'd followed her in. He was a weakness for her, and if she wanted to survive, she'd need to set boundaries and tell him to stay away.

Thoughts of what she'd read earlier flooded her mind. She spun toward him, words on her lips when they were stolen by his. The kiss fanned her emotions until they erupted at his hunger and need. In that moment, the rawness clouded some things but made others perfectly clear.

She wanted him here and now. No matter how much it would screw up everything that was already a mess. She wanted Damien, even though she wouldn't keep him. She wanted this memory for all the lonely days and nights ahead.

So when he lifted her, she clung to him. When her back hit her bed, her body quivered with longing. Seeing the stark need on his face, his gaze riveted to her body, she felt his desire echoing in her own. It was overwhelming. Did it have anything to do with the bite? She didn't know. But between those thoughts, her pants had disappeared, and his mouth was on her pussy, only the barrier of her lace keeping them apart.

That her first time would be with a man she barely knew felt somehow right. She should tell him she was inexperienced, but then his lips did something to her clit, and she screamed. The orgasm launched her to another stratosphere. Even when she'd touched herself in the dark of her room, it had never felt like this.

Everything around her was cloaked in sexuality. Her body charged yet heavy. Her eyelids lifted to see Damien naked at the edge of the bed, and holy hell, she drank in the sight of him.

She'd never seen a man naked in real life—movies and such, but never like this. She was pretty sure Damien was a god among men. She swept her gaze downward from his blue eyes to his chest, her breath halting at the size of his manhood.

A chill ran over her as he moved, crawling along her body, the rest of her clothes suddenly gone. She wanted to ask how, but his lips swallowed that thought again, and she tasted herself.

When had her legs parted? She didn't know. But she felt him there at her core, his cock thick and swollen, her hips urging him to move. And he did. Pressure so intense as he joined their bodies, just barely.

She felt stretched and full. Every stroke took him deeper until pleasure and pain coursed through her, the mark on her shoulder burning as he claimed her virginity.

She never knew it could be like this, that she could be like this. She grabbed onto him wherever she could reach, moans being ripped from her chest, his name on constant repeat. She was racing toward a cliff at frightening speed but would never stop.

Damien pulled out of her and flipped her to her front, his cock finding her again, the assault harder this time. She couldn't keep up with him, ripples starting one after the other from her womb and exploding through her, throwing her over the edge as she heard her name echoed from behind her, where he bucked and cursed. The heat of his chest pressed against her back as he tugged her in tightly.

The douse of cold reality hit as he spoke, his demand to move in with him crushing what they had just shared. And if he called her Peach one more time, she was going to throw whatever was nearest at his head.

"That's the second time I've heard that word 'mated' today. I'm saying no to it and you." Her anger was a seething entity inside her.

And then Damien changed into a monster. A real-life monster. He looked ugly and violent, her scream ricocheting off the walls as she turned to run, and he grabbed her. Her entire being shifted into panic mode at his unrecognizable voice, telling her that he was a monster. There was more, but she couldn't think.

In another blink, she was with a stunned Kimora and Bane from the birthday party. She took refuge with the other woman while listening as Damien reappeared and barked orders about her life, her mind trying to grasp everything being thrown at her. Kimora seemed to be in her corner until the bite mark was revealed and shared.

Her world had just tilted off its axis because of some stupid bite. But screw Damien. She wasn't going to be put into another cage or follow someone else's rules—never again. She'd lost years of her life under Donovan's thumb. One thing he'd learn soon enough was how street smart she was.

What he'd turned into was terrifying. Could Donovan do that, too? She gave Bane and Kimora a side-eye, wondering what they were. Was she the only normal one here? Giving that a second thought, she wasn't entirely normal, but she didn't have an alter ego like he did.

Sadie stayed quiet while the others seemed to agree on her fate. Patience—she had that in spades. She'd gather as much information as she could, then make her move. Screw him, them, and all this mate bullshit. She was deciding her own fate.

Chapter 19

Kimora asked Bane to show Sadie their spare bedroom that came complete with an inviting bathroom suite while she gathered a few things, laying out a plush robe, a few soft bath towels, all the little comforts she thought Sadie would need to feel at home.

But as she arranged the items, her thoughts drifted back to the first time she met Bane. At that moment, she had been fiercely stubborn, pushing him away with every fiber of her being. Like Damien, she had convinced herself that she didn't deserve the love of a hellhound. Her past had been a tangled path, one that led her away from her father, and it certainly didn't include the fierce affection of a creature like Bane.

"If you need anything else Sadie, please come find us." Pulling her in for a quick hug, Bane already headed down the hall, then she closed the door behind her, giving her some quiet time.

Entering the kitchen, her mate's presence filled the room with warmth, and she walked into his open arms. His strength was everything she needed. His lips found her neck, pressing tender kisses there. "What's on your mind, mo ghrá?" he murmured, his voice rich with that thick Scottish accent that still made her knees weak.

Kimora leaned into his embrace, resting her head against his broad chest. Though she towered at 5'10", in his arms, she felt small and cherished. Bane was a formidable 6'10", his thick black locks cascading down to frame a rugged face adorned with a full beard. His chestnut eyes held a depth that seemed to draw her in, captivating her endlessly. He was beyond handsome. He was the embodiment of her deepest desires, and that accent made her heart race every damn time.

"I was thinking about how stubborn I was when I first met you," she admitted, her voice catching slightly. "How I almost walked away from the love of my life simply because I didn't think I deserved your love." She wiped away the tears that had begun to trickle down her cheeks, the weight of those memories still sharp.

"Bhí tú beagán stubborn, agus bhí sé de dhíth ar Damien chun tú a dhéanamh a fheiceáil go raibh ár ngrá fiúntach troid," Bane replied gently, his Gaelic words rolling off his tongue like a soothing melody. "Aye, ye were a wee bit stubborn, lass. It took Damien tae mak' ye see that our love was worth fightin' fer."

He cupped her face in his hands, his expression growing serious. "Ah think we need tae tell Sadie the truth about Damien. He might be a right arsehole sometimes, but we baith ken his love knows nae bounds, an' he'll do whatever it takes tae protect his family. Let's go tae bed, lass," he added, taking her hand in his, his grip steady and reassuring as he led her toward their bedroom. The day had been long and exhausting, but in his presence, she found her center again.

---

The morning sun filtered through the curtains, casting a warm glow in the bedroom as Kimora stirred awake. She turned to find Bane propped up on one elbow, his chestnut eyes watching her with an intensity that made her heart flutter. Today was the day they had promised to tell Sadie the truth—the truth about Damien.

They showered together like they did most mornings, stealing moments where they could because they'd almost lost each other centuries ago. Her silent vow to always let Bane know how much she loved him played through her mind as his hands moved gently through her hair.

After a quick breakfast, they gathered in the living room, where Sadie sat curled up on the couch, her curiosity evident in her expressive eyes. Kimora exchanged a glance with Bane, and he nodded, encouraging her to begin.

"Sadie," Kimora started, her voice steady but soft, "we need to talk to you about Damien. There's something you should know."

Bane leaned closer, his presence a comforting weight beside her. "Damien isnae just family; he's the god of monsters. He's our King," he added, his tone serious yet filled with affection. "And his story is one o' baith great love and heartbreakin' loss."

Sadie's brow furrowed as she looked between them. "What do you mean?"

Kimora took a deep breath, her chest tight. "Damien was once mated to a woman he believed he would be with forever. He loved her with all his heart, and together they had a beautiful baby boy." Her voice softened as she spoke of the child, remembering how Damien's eyes used to light up when he talked about his son. "He was over the moon happy; he had everything he ever wanted."

"But," Bane interjected, his jaw clenching, "there was somethin' off aboot Damien's wife. We could sense it, but Damien wouldnae hear a word against her. His love blinded him tae the truth."

Kimora's heart ached as she continued. "The betrayal that followed was unimaginable. One day, his wife took their precious son, filled the tub with water, and..." She couldn't finish the sentence. The horror of it stuck in her throat.

"She drowned him," Bane said quietly. "He was just three months auld."

The silence that followed was deafening. Sadie's hand flew to her mouth, tears welling in her eyes. "How could she do that?"

Bane's expression hardened, his protective nature surfacing. "Love can be a powerful t'ing, but so can betrayal. Ze loss shattered Damien and eet changed heem forever. He needs us, an' he needs ye to understand the darkness he carries."

Kimora reached out, gently squeezing Sadie's hand. "We're telling you this because we want you to know that even in the depths of despair, there is still a family here who loves you. Damien may be a god, but he's also a father who lost everything."

She could see it then—the way Sadie's expression shifted from horror to understanding to something deeper. The girl was in love with Damien; she couldn't hide it if she tried. With one obstacle out of the way, Kimora turned her attention to the mating mark.

"Sadie," Kimora said gently, "I know you're upset about the mark Damien gave you." She paused, watching as Sadie's hand moved instinctively to her shoulder. "Let me show you mine."

Kimora lifted her sleeve to reveal a series of intricate paw prints etched into her skin, intertwined with Celtic knots that seemed to shimmer in the morning light. "This is my mating mark," she explained, her voice tender yet firm. "It represents my connection to Bane. It's like a wedding ring for humans—a promise of love and protection."

Bane leaned in closer, his voice warm and rich with that Scottish lilt that made everything sound like poetry. "No other lad can touch a mated lass, ken? It's a symbol of our love and loyalty," he said, his eyes earnest as they met Sadie's. "You're safe, Sadie. You're part of our family now."

Sadie stared at the mark, then back at their faces. "He chose me?"

"Aye, lass," Bane said softly. "His soul chose ye, even if his mind is still catchin' up."

# Chapter 20

She just wanted to be alone, yet at the same time, not entirely alone. And at that realization, Sadie knew she was screwed. Because she'd always liked being alone—alone meant safety. That's how she knew Damien was different. Even with everything that had happened, there was this yearning to be with him, to have him close.

When he'd turned and left her alone with Bane and Kimora, his holier-than-thou attitude mixed with that insufferable smugness, she'd wanted to grab the nearest object and hurl it at his oversized head. But the couple's home was filled with timeless pieces, and Sadie could never damage a piece of history. Every item held a story. In her mind though, she'd smacked him upside his large ego—hard.

Her body and her mind felt the loss of him. How was that even possible? Even after Bane and Kimora had left her alone, she'd showered, the warmth easing her muscles, soothing the soreness between her legs. Her eyes had drifted shut under the spray, and suddenly she was with him again. The rasp of his breath at her ear, his touch along the underside of her breasts, his mouth on her clit. Her hips arched, searching for him, wanting his cock buried deep within her again.

Her mark flared, burned a hot path down from her shoulder to her spine, then lower to her back. She was going to push herself over the edge just by thinking of him. His bite had changed her—how else could she explain what was happening to her? Her mind created the most erotic daydream, and all she could do was lean back against the tiles and let her fingertips find her swollen bud, stroking herself to release until she bit her lower lip to stay quiet.

Kimora was right. She was fucked. She wanted him, but she didn't want to want him. Damien was a risk, a huge risk to her life. He should have been wrapped in caution tape—not that she would have heeded it.

Exhaustion replaced her arousal. The room they'd offered her called to her now, the bed already turned down and waiting. She'd sleep and decide in the morning how to escape. It occurred to her that her purse and phone were still at her apartment.

Barely drying off, she slipped between the sheets, sighing at the softness of the high thread count. Tomorrow. Tomorrow, she'd reclaim her life.

---

Sadie knew by the glances Bane and Kimora exchanged, and the way their gazes touched on her, then back to each other, that something was up. She could feel it the moment she walked into the kitchen.

"Thank you both for the clothes and the bed. I feel more myself this morning." A cup of coffee appeared, pushed her way. She knew it would be rude just to bolt out the door, and besides, she'd have to call an Uber to get back to her place. Then a plate of eggs and toast was set before her, and she didn't have the heart to say the coffee alone would have been fine.

It was the softness in Kimora's voice and the way her doe eyes reflected her emotions that made Sadie realize more was coming. When Bane claimed his place next to his wife, the breakfast she'd just forced herself to eat sat like a stone in her stomach. The plush sofa offered no comfort.

Then they both dropped it all on her—a short, heartbreaking biography of Damien Nikolas. She still couldn't comprehend the god or king part, even after seeing what he'd transformed into. Her brain couldn't wrap itself around this hidden world she'd fallen into. That he'd lost a child by the hands of the mother was the most horrific thing she'd ever heard. She couldn't even begin to imagine the pain or how you moved on with your life after such a tragedy.

They'd been intimate, they'd touched, they'd fucked. *Made love* came to mind, but it hadn't been that. It was more animalistic. Yet even with all that closeness, her hands caressing every part of him, not one vision had appeared. Maybe because of who and what he was? She knew she wouldn't want to feel that, though. The anguish of a child's death would tear her apart. That was Damien's secret, his grief to share with those he chose.

Kimora's touch was gentle and caring. Sadie liked her and Bane. Damien was lucky to have friends like them—they had his back. At Kimora's reveal of her own mating mark, Sadie wanted to ask what hers would reveal, what mark would represent Damien, but she couldn't go there yet. She needed time alone to process the last couple of days.

Bane's reassurance that she was safe brought a soft smile to her lips as she lifted her gaze to each of them in turn, Kimora's hand still joined with hers. "Bane, I really do appreciate everything you've both done for me. A lot is going on in my life, and I need time to figure out a few things. I will be leaving here today, though. Damien can't keep me here like a prisoner. He's not the boss of me." That sounded utterly ridiculous even to her own ears.

Kimora's squeeze to her hand drew her eyes downward to the intricate bracelet she wore, so delicate against the golden hue of her skin.

"Kimora, this is beautiful." Sadie's other hand lifted, gently running the pad of her finger over the markings etched in each linked piece, not even thinking...

*"Princess, you must get your rest." The softest golds formed a backdrop where a young woman stood, her face blotchy from crying. Sand dunes were chiseled with ripples, the effect like ocean waves reflecting in the moonlight.*

*"Amar, I will. Everything will change with the rising of the sun, and I just want to remember today, so I will always remember how I felt." Her profile was regal, her gaze distant, while her fingers stroked something she held within her hands.*

*"Your parents' death will be avenged. I have scouts out hunting at our borders. Princess Kimora, we must get you inside behind the palace walls. You are our future."*

*Her long fall of chestnut hair shone even without the company of the sun. Sadie would have known it was her, even without the guard saying her name.*

*"Amar, would you place this on my wrist for me?" His bow was full of pride, if Sadie read his face correctly.*

*"Your mama would be so proud of you." His hands gently lifted the bracelet from her open palm. "But princess, there is still some..." He didn't*

*need to finish the sentence. Dried blood coated several of the links and the clasp. Sadie was grateful she hadn't envisioned more.*

*"Leave it. I'll wear my mama's blood with pride. No one strikes out against the House of Seti and lives."*

---

"Sadie? Sadie?" Bane's deep brogue splintered her vision, his concern etched around his eyes as she slowly refocused on the here and now.

She released Kimora's hand, running her palms along the tops of her thighs. "I'm okay. Sorry for my..." She left that thought dangling.

"Whit just happened, lass?" The look on his face was one she'd seen many times.

"Sadie, you looked like you were miles away." Kimora reached for her again, and Sadie stood, giving herself some space while deciding what to say.

They'd both been genuine with her, offering their home and friendship. She couldn't give them any less.

"Your bracelet told me a story. I'm sorry for the loss of your parents. Your mama would love the woman you've become. Did Amar ever find out who took them from you?"

Silence.

Two sets of eyes froze on her, mouths open. She waited.

"How did you know that, Sadie? That's impossible. Only Bane knows that this was my mama's."

"I see things sometimes by touch. I can't always control it, and I never know if it will be good or bad. Most times it's bad, even horrific. It can happen with objects or clothing, or just a simple skin-on-skin touch. Sometimes I'm flung into a vision almost painfully, while other times it's more of a slow drift. It's happened my whole life." Her shoulders lifted in a slight shrug, scared to look directly at them. She spoke more to the wall behind them.

Then Bane's Scottish drawl pulled her eyes his way. "Does Damien know?"

She shook her head. "No. He kind of just jumped to the biting part. We don't know each other at all. This is all just a mess." Her anxiety started to build. "I need to leave. I need to figure this all out. Donovan will be looking for me, too. Don't tell Damien I've left. Please."

She'd never forget Kimora's face at that moment. "Sadie? Damien's our friend and our king. He's yours as you are his. We have to tell him. Your safety must come first. You don't understand this yet, but he's very powerful and has his own enemies who would think nothing to hurt you to get to him. No one knows you're marked but us. But when they do? And that will happen—you'll need to have guards. But it's not as bad as it sounds. I rarely see mine because they are just that good at keeping to the shadows. He has to know. And you both need to talk about everything. But you have time. Bane and I won't say a thing. It's just our secret."

"He knows. Donovan knows. He saw the mark. He knew it was Damien's." Sadie's thoughts spun out of control as she realized she might have just fallen down a rabbit hole.

"Och, fuck." Bane's declaration summed it all up.

# Chapter 21

The serpent mark on Damien's neck flared to life, heat shooting through the intricate scales etched into his skin. Miles away, Sadie would be experiencing the same burning sensation—their bond crackling with the intensity of his emotions. He pressed his fingertips against the mark, deliberately sending another wave of fire coursing toward his mate.

She needed to understand. They were connected, bound by something deeper than flesh and blood. He would tear apart anyone who threatened her, even if that meant protecting her from her own reckless determination. Donovan's hands would never touch a single golden strand of her hair—not while Damien still drew breath.

The bastard thought he could hide his operation within the city's shadows, but his contract had expired. The hourglass had run empty, and sand had scattered to the wind.

Donovan—a lesser demon with delusions of godhood. If Damien gave the word, his father's Scottish hound would drag the pretender to the bile-stained depths of Tartarus, where he'd rot for eternity in chains of his own making.

No escape. No mercy. Damien would ensure it.

"What's on your mind, hellhound?" Damien's eyebrow arched as Bane walked in, his expression guarded, something darker flickering behind the hound's eyes.

Bane's weathered hand scraped down his beard—that telltale gesture he used when treading on dangerous ground. "I think ye need tae have a word wi' Sadie. Be honest wi' her—tell her how ye really feel. Let her know the truth about Donovan an' why she needs tae stick wi' Kimora an' me."

Damien's exhale came slow and controlled, but his pulse hammered against his throat. "There's more you're not telling me." His voice dropped to that dangerous register that made lesser demons flee. "You're my brother in all but blood, Bane. You think I can't smell a half-truth on you?"

The hellhound's jaw tightened. "Ah made a promise tae Sadie that ah wudnae tell ye. That ah wud give her that chance tae tell ye herself. So dinnae ask me tae break it."

Damien's respect for Bane's loyalty warred with his frustration. The hound's honor ran bone-deep—one of the reasons Damien trusted him with his life. "Will I want to hear what she has to say?"

"Let's just say, ye'll ken why Donovan keeps her close."

Rage erupted through Damien's veins like molten lava. His vision bled red at the edges, and his hands clenched into fists that could shatter stone. The monster inside him pressed against his ribs, clawing for release.

He raked his fingers through his hair, each strand catching between his knuckles as he fought the beast threatening to tear free. Every muscle in his body coiled tight, ready to spring.

Images flashed—Donovan's leering face, his hands reaching for Sadie, his voice whispering poisoned words in her ear.

Control. He needed control, or everything would burn.

"Can you bring Sadie here?" His voice came out rougher than intended. "If things get heated, you can step in."

Bane jingled his keys, that familiar grin spreading across his weathered features. "Aye, nae bother, boss. If things go a wee bit awry, just mind that I'm no the enemy."

…

The door opened, and Sadie's citrus scent hit him like a physical blow. Sweet oranges and summer sunshine flooded his senses, making his mouth water and his pulse spike. The room transformed—suddenly brighter, warmer, alive with her presence.

Her golden hair caught the light streaming through the windows, each strand gleaming like spun sunlight around her face. She moved with that fluid grace that never failed to steal his breath, strength, and femininity woven together in perfect harmony.

His mating mark throbbed in response to her nearness, heat spreading through his chest and down his arms. The world narrowed to just her—everything else faded to white noise as their bond hummed with electric possibility.

Bane chuckled, shaking his head. "Ah'm gonnae gie ye two some privacy. I'll be in the livin' room if ye need me."

Silence stretched between them like a taut wire, ready to snap. Damien broke it first, his voice cutting through the tension. "I know how we left things, but I won't apologize for wanting to keep you safe." His eyes searched hers, pleading for understanding even as frustration bled through his carefully controlled tone.

Sadie's arms crossed over her chest, her glare sharp enough to draw blood. "You know you can be a real ass, Damien." Each word cracked like a whip. "You realize you made my life more complicated than it already was?"

The monster inside him stirred, pressing against his self-control. His eyes darkened, pupils dilating as he hissed his response. "Do you realize how dangerous Donovan is? Do you even know what he is?" Urgency thrummed through every syllable.

She stared at him as if he'd grown a second head, disbelief painted across her features. "Is he a monster like you?" Her anger flared white-hot, challenging him to his core.

Damien leaned back against the kitchen counter, arms crossed in a mirror of her defensive posture. His knuckles whitened as he gripped his own forearms. "I'm not hiding what I am, Peach. You've seen my true face." His voice remained steady, but intensity radiated from every line of his body. "Donovan is the worst kind of monster—he takes without asking and doesn't care who bleeds as long as he gets what he wants. The fact that you're still breathing means he needs something from you." His words hung in the air like a blade, waiting to fall. "What does he want, Sadie?"

# *Chapter 22*

Mental exhaustion crashed over Sadie like a tidal wave, driving her legs toward her room after her conversation with Kimora and Bane. Her mind reeled—they were kind, welcoming, and completely inhuman. The knowledge sat heavy in her chest, a weight she couldn't shake.

An entire world of beings walked among them, breathing the same air, sharing the same streets, and she'd been blind to it all. Or had she? Her steps faltered as memories surfaced—years of strange sensations, whispered warnings from her sixth sense that she'd deliberately silenced. She'd chosen the comfortable darkness of ignorance over the harsh light of truth.

But the Band-Aid had been torn away now, taking skin with it. Her new reality demanded action, ready or not.

The low murmur of voices drifted from the other room—Bane and Kimora discussing her fate, no doubt. She pressed her ear to the door, straining to catch fragments of their conversation, but her frustratingly human hearing caught only unintelligible whispers.

The visions from Kimora's bracelet haunted her—centuries of memories flooding through her touch. Kimora looked twenty-five but had lived for hundreds of years. Which meant Damien... Her stomach clenched. Kimora called him their king. A king needed a kingdom, a throne, and subjects. Where did a demon king rule? Earth? Or somewhere else entirely?

The mattress dipped as she collapsed onto the bed, her skull pounding with information it couldn't process. Anyone she confided in would have her committed. This was the stuff of dark romance novels—the kind she devoured in secret, never imagining she'd become the heroine of her own impossible story.

Her mark erupted with sudden warmth, heat cascading down her spine and radiating outward through her limbs. Her muscles loosened, tension melting away like ice in sunlight. Damien's doing? Would this become her new normal—his emotions bleeding into hers without warning?

She let her eyes drift closed, sinking into the mattress as his presence filled every corner of her consciousness. She felt him everywhere—his hands gripping her hips with bruising intensity, his mouth claiming hers with desperate hunger, his body moving against hers with primal need. Her thighs clenched involuntarily, her body betraying her with its fierce response.

She didn't want to want him. But somewhere between one breath and the next, he'd crawled under her skin, infected her blood, made himself essential. Their intimacy clung to her like perfume, following her every movement. She was drowning in a whirlpool of her own making, pulled under by currents she couldn't fight.

He was a monster—literally, factually, undeniably. And the most intoxicating man she'd ever encountered.

The ceiling stared back at her, offering no answers as she faced the crossroads of her life. Every path led to danger, but staying still meant certain death. She had to choose. She had to reclaim her life, piece by broken piece.

A knock shattered her spiral of thoughts. Bane's rich accent penetrated the door, bringing an unexpected smile to her lips despite everything.

She dragged herself from the bed and opened the door to find his concerned tawny eyes studying her face.

"Sadie lass, Damien wants tae hae a wee blether wi' ye. Ah've no' said a word tae him aboot anythin'." His weathered hands twisted together. "Ah can tell ye he's the best friend ah've got. He's a decent lad, even if he can be a bit of an eejit at times. Would ye gie him a chance?"

Love and respect colored every word when Bane spoke of Damien—the kind of bond forged in fire and blood, tested by time and never found wanting. Her body made the decision before her mind caught up. She nodded, the movement barely perceptible but unmistakably there.

The drive passed in comfortable silence, Bane's steady presence a balm to her frayed nerves. She liked him—genuinely, deeply. Kimora was lucky to have found him, and Sadie suspected their love story would be worth hearing someday. But first, she had to sort out her own tangled mess.

The moment Damien came into view, her body ignited. Her mark flared to life, sending heat racing through her veins, and somewhere in the back of her mind, she registered that something felt different. Changed. Like a door had been opened that could never be closed again.

Bane's parting words barely registered as he left them alone. Damien's voice filled the space, reverent and stubborn and concerned all at once. She understood his protective instincts, even appreciated them, but she wouldn't trade one cage for another, no matter how gilded.

She didn't know where this path led, what his world contained, or if she'd survive the journey. But his emotions flowed through their bond like a river—care, devotion, fear for her safety. Raw honesty that couldn't be faked or hidden. He deserved the same from her.

Her legs carried her to the kitchen table without conscious thought. She sank into a chair, hands folded in her lap, searching for words that seemed too small for the truth she carried.

"I met Donovan when I was seventeen and living on the streets." The words scraped her throat raw. Damien abandoned his position against the counter, sliding into the chair across from her, his full attention a weight she felt in her bones. "I saved his life, and he took me in. Put me through school, gave me a job, made me feel safe." Her fingers twisted together, a nervous habit she'd never broken. "Since I was little, I could see things through touch. History unfolding—good and bad. Donovan uses me as a lie detector and an investment. I've made him millions over the years."

She should have left long ago. Should have found the courage to break free. But fear had kept her chained more effectively than any lock.

"So he's blackmailing you." Damien's eyes darkened, pupils dilating until they swallowed the color. A low rage thrummed through their bond, making her own pulse spike in response.

"In a way." The admission tasted bitter. "He gave me everything—education, security, purpose. I owed him. Or I thought I did. But Donovan always wants more. He even flew in a specialist to study my psychometry—that's what it's called. Apparently, it's rare and unpredictable." The realization hit her like a physical blow. "He's never going to let me go, Damien. Not without a fight. I've been gathering evidence against him for months, but if he's like you... No human prison could hold him."

Tears blurred her vision as Damien's fury blazed through their connection like wildfire.

"I don't want anyone hurt because of me." Her voice cracked, betraying the fear she'd tried so hard to hide. "I know you're some kind of god, but Donovan has power too. And I love my job at the museum." Her hands flew to her arms, rubbing frantically as heat built under her skin. "Damien, are you doing this? I feel like I'm going to explode."

# Chapter 23

Damien's fists collided with the countertop as he stood from the table and turned, rage like thunder, the ancient wood splintering beneath his knuckles. Cracks spider-webbed across the surface as his rage erupted—a living thing with teeth and claws, demanding Donovan's blood.

"Calm yerself, boss." Bane materialized beside him, his heavy hand settling on Damien's shoulder like an anchor in a storm. "Ye don't want to frighten her. Sadie came here to be honest wi' ye."

The monster inside Damien clawed at his ribs, desperate for release. His vision bled red at the edges, every muscle coiled to spring. "I'm losing control, Bane. That bastard held her hostage in her own mind, and I want to paint the walls with his entrails."

Bane's weathered face creased with understanding. "Aye, I ken that. But we need tae focus. Sadie's scared. She needs tae know she's safe—that we can handle whatever Donovan throws at us."

Damien's gaze found Sadie across the room, tears threatening to spill from her luminous eyes. His heart cracked like glass. She was stronger than titanium, but Donovan had kept her wrapped in shadows for too long.

"Lu me tesoro," he whispered, crossing to her on silent feet. His hands enveloped hers, their mating marks pulsing in synchrony—two hearts beating as one. "No one will get hurt. Not you, not Bane, not Kimora. We'll figure this out together."

Vulnerability painted her features in watercolors of fear and hope. "I don't always understand my visions. Sometimes they're so random, and it terrifies me."

"Then let's explore it together." His voice steadied, becoming the foundation she could build her courage upon. "Bane can guide you through a vision. With his powers, he can create roadmaps. You just have to learn how to see them. Trust me—you can do this."

Bane stepped forward, his presence a shield against the unknown. "Aye, lass. Let me help ye connect to my energy. It might give ye a clearer picture of what ye can do."

Sadie's hesitation lasted only a heartbeat before she nodded. "Okay. I can try. But I'm not going to lie. I'm scared."

"That's ok, Sadie. We've all been where you are now. Unsure what our powers can do. And that's what you have—a power. Donovan has just been misusing it." Damien's voice calmed her and settled her jumping nerves.

Bane pulled a chair up next to hers, taking her hand in his, palm to palm. Damien watched every micro-expression cross her face, ready to catch her if she fell. "Close your eyes," he instructed, his voice honey-smooth. "Breathe deeply and let the energy flow."

The moment Sadie's eyelids fluttered shut, the atmosphere shifted. Her stomach plummeted as reality fractured around her, pulling her into another realm entirely.

The vision bloomed behind her closed eyes—Bane, decades younger, standing at the precipice of a wasteland where hope went to die. Tension crackled through the air like electricity, and shadows writhed in the distance with malevolent purpose. Then transformation claimed him—muscles rippling, bones reshaping, until a magnificent hellhound stood where the man had been. His midnight fur absorbed light, his ember eyes blazing with otherworldly fire.

"Bloody hell," she breathed, awe and pride warring in her chest. Bane's first transformation was poetry written in violence, but beauty always came with a price.

"Bane, no!" The cry tore from her throat as the vision deepened.

She felt his empathy like a physical weight, for the lost soul flickering in the darkness, fighting a battle it had already lost. The soul's cries echoed through dimensions, a symphony of despair that made her bones ache.

"Dinnae worry, lass," Bane's voice resonated through the vision, determination forging each word into steel. "I have to do this. It's my duty." His growl shook the earth before he lunged forward, consuming the soul in holy fire.

Sadie flinched as her heart shattered for both the soul and the man who carried such burdens. Bane's voice anchored her to the present. "Focus on that feeling, Sadie. What does it tell ye?"

The vision shifted like smoke, revealing Bane as a guardian, watching over innocents with fierce devotion, his expression softening with compassion that ran deeper than oceans.

"He's not just a hellhound," she murmured, understanding dawning like sunrise. "He's a protector, bound to darkness but fighting for light."

Pride swelled in Damien's chest until he thought it might burst. "Bane's strength comes from loyalty—his willingness to bear others' burdens."

The battlefield materialized around them next—chaos incarnate, where steel sang death songs and warriors screamed their last breaths. Bane stood at the center like an immovable monument, hellhound and guardian angel wrapped in one fierce package. Unease flickered through Sadie as the magnitude of his battles crashed over her.

"Don't fear the vision, lass," Bane's voice cut through her anxiety like a blade through silk. "Aye, it can be daunting, but remember—I'm here to protect ye. Focus on the strength within ye, not the darkness around us."

Damien's encouragement joined the chorus. "You've got this, Sadie. Look at Bane—he's not just shadow and flame. He fights for light, and so can you."

As Bane launched into battle with a growl that shook dimensions, admiration flooded Sadie's veins despite her fear. "He carries the weight of their souls, doesn't he?"

"Aye," Bane's response resonated with raw emotion. "But ye needn't carry that burden alone, Sadie. Together, we'll face whatever comes."

Sadie's eyes opened, her body melting into relaxation. Damien cupped her face, his palms warm against her skin. "Mi Tesoro, do you see why Donovan keeps you close? He doesn't care about you—only what you can do for him. Once he gets what he wants, he'll kill you. This is why you need to move here with me, where I can protect you."

…

Damien's explosion had Sadie leaping from her chair, his emotions crashing through their bond like a tsunami. Every wave of his fury battered her already fragile control. Managing her own emotional storms was a challenge enough without adding his tempest to the mix.

Bane's soothing presence wrapped around her frayed nerves like a warm blanket. She watched Damien wage war with himself, every thought etched in the sharp angles of his face. If Donovan materialized in this room, there wouldn't be enough left of him to identify.

A lifetime of visions had shown her enough violence to fill a thousand nightmares. She couldn't bear being the catalyst for more bloodshed. Maybe that's why she'd stayed in Donovan's gilded cage so long—fear of who might pay the price if she ran. Collateral damage seemed to follow in his wake like a faithful dog. Or maybe that was just another excuse for her own cowardice.

But since meeting Damien and his friends, hope had taken root in the wasteland of her heart.

Through her blur of tears—and damn her body and its constant leaking—she watched Damien approach. His endearment wrapped around her like silk, and her hands clutched his like a drowning woman grasping driftwood. Their connection defied logic, but she couldn't deny its pull.

No one had ever offered to help her understand her gift before. Donovan only demanded she use it, willing or not, like a tool to be picked up and discarded.

Despite knowing them for mere days, safety bloomed in their presence. Safe enough to walk into visions with their guidance, to let them stand guard while she explored the labyrinth of her abilities. With their supernatural strength as her shield, maybe she could finally master the visions instead of being their victim.

What Bane shared touched her soul—his trust a precious gift she'd guard fiercely, just as he protected her secrets. And Damien had stood sentinel beside her, his support unwavering, his encouragement a lifeline. She'd never had this before—this warmth, this circle of belonging.

But ice water doused her budding hope at his next words. Move in with him. From one cage to another, no matter how beautiful the bars.

"Stop." She yanked her hands free, putting necessary distance between them. "I appreciate everything you've all done. I know better than anyone what Donovan's capable of—maybe more so now that I understand the supernatural element. But Damien, I can't just disappear. I owe him a conversation, and I want to keep my job at the museum." Her laugh came out brittle. "Though that's probably wishful thinking, isn't it? Once I leave, everything gets left behind."

Her gaze bounced between the two men. "I have feelings for you, but this has happened so fast, I need time. We don't even know each other." Her voice began to fracture. "I don't know your favorite color or movie, and I know that sounds stupid, but none of this is normal." She drew a deep breath, squaring her shoulders like armor. "Take me back to my place. Tomorrow I'm going to talk to Donovan. I have insurance hidden away for this moment. He'll see reason—he has to. Then I can walk away on my own terms, and we can explore whatever this is between us."

She stood there, watching something dangerous bloom across Damien's features.

…

Damien's hands clenched into weapons at his sides as he glared between her and Bane. "You don't understand! This isn't about wanting your old life back. You're my mate—protecting you is written into my very DNA!"

Bane moved closer, his voice steady despite the thick Scottish burr. "Aye, I feel yer pain, mate. But ye cannae push her like that. It'll only drive her deeper into danger, aye? She needs to feel she has agency over her own life, even if it terrifies ye."

Fire erupted in Damien's eyes. "You should understand my fury, Bane! I'm fighting for her life, and you act like I'm being unreasonable. This isn't some fucking game to me!"

Sadie's heart hammered against her ribs as she looked between them. "I just want my life back. I didn't ask for this world. All of this is drowning me." Her voice trembled under the weight of their expectations.

Damien's expression softened fractionally as he met her eyes, but when he turned back to Bane, frustration boiled over like lava. "What if she gets hurt? What if that bastard Donovan manipulates her or holds something over her head to keep her chained to him? I can't bear losing her to the very monster I'm meant to protect her from. I would burn this world to ash for her. I'd kill Donovan without blinking."

## Chapter 24

The others were late, or maybe he was early. His day had started behind the eight ball and twisted out of shape since. Even the woman who shared his bed hadn't wanted to leave.

He'd smeared on his usual charm with a promise of a jewelry store visit later in the week, finally watching her backside disappear through the front door. What the hell had he been thinking? He hadn't.

Anger and alcohol had carried him to bed the night before. Not a single member of his team could find where Sadie had disappeared. Hours and countless resources spent hunting her down after she fled the elevator, his emotions running the gamut because of that damn mark.

His first thought—that Damien Nikolas had done it to mess with him and his empire—gave way to common sense. If jealous spite had motivated the action, the situation would be easier to handle. But at first glance of the mark, it couldn't lie. The mark pulsed in various shades, emboldened and real. Damien had found his mate, and his mate happened to be his Sadie.

The rage churned in his gut again because she was his. Everything she had become was because of him. He didn't care if he had to cut the damn thing off her—she was staying with him.

He shifted in the high-backed chair he'd claimed thirty minutes earlier. One hand gripped his tumbler of whiskey while the fingers of his other hand played with a centuries-old coin, his gaze fixed on the two-way mirror.

The Dungeon was his baby—a high-end men's club, slightly archaic in nature, but he didn't give a shit. Sex was a business like anything else. He ran it legitimately, to a point. Like his other above-board investments, he showed profit and paid taxes.

Flipping the coin in the air and catching it—two sides, two-faced. Everyone was. Donovan had never met anyone who couldn't be bought or coerced to his side. His underground portfolio proved that: drugs, loan sharking, and enforcement. If it made money, he wanted a piece.

And that's why he wasn't letting go of Sadie. She made him wealthy. Her touch was worth its weight in gold, and he wasn't giving up that gold mine.

California was a large territory. They all had their pieces of the pie. Why Damien had decided to interfere in his world remained unclear, but he'd been aware of him pushing boundaries for a while. To be honest, at least with himself, he mostly stayed out of Damien's crosshairs. He'd heard enough rumors over time to know who to mess with and who not to. But with recent events, those bets were off.

A knock, then the door to his office opened on a whisper from behind him. "Boss, Drake sent me. He said he tried calling you, but you didn't answer."

Goddamn. He set down his drink, patting his pockets. Where the hell had he left his phone? "What's wrong?"

"Sadie returned to her place, but Mr. Nikolas showed up. Then nothing. They never left. The boys were watching, but Drake says he knows for a fact they aren't in there."

He pushed to his feet, facing Burke. "When were they last seen?"

"Last night. Nothing since."

His insides boiled. Drake was a mixed demon breed. If he couldn't sense them inside her walls, it meant Damien had taken her elsewhere—the demon way. Sadie was being tutored on the dark side, which enraged him more. He'd always been so gentle with her, keeping her unaware. Well, fuck everyone! The problem now was that Damien wouldn't let her out of his sight, whether his own or his goons.

"Tell the boys to get back here now." Realization dawned— he'd left his phone in his car, parked at the casino, because he'd been too inebriated and filled with lust to drive. Even if Drake had reached him, there would have been nothing he could have done with Damien in-house. Time for a new strategy.

---

"Sadie, lass, how Damien feels aboot ye is how I feel aboot Kimora. We cannae fight the matin' or its urges, ken. It's a part o' us like our blood an' breath, so it is."

Bane's words spun on a carousel in her head, even hours after he'd dropped her at her place. That Damien had let her go even after his meltdown showed how he was willing to consider her wants and needs, but they came with strings.

Someone from his team would always be around. If she needed him, he would come ASAP. When she finished talking to Donovan, he expected a call, and then he was taking her away for a bit so they could connect and talk.

She peeked through her front blinds. The setting sun cast her street in shadows, but there was no mistaking the black Land Rover with the serious man sitting in the driver's seat, staring straight at her. Bane had said his name was Enzo. If she looked out the back, there would be a replica black Land Rover with Levi at the wheel.

Ice cream.

She needed ice cream and a firm talk with herself to get her personal compass back to True North—hers had been bent for a while. She might be angry at how this had transpired with Damien and his bite, but it had also made her fully wake up to what her life had become.

She stepped away from the window, taking a straight line to the fridge. Pulling open the bottom drawer, the Ben & Jerry's label stared up at her—rocky road was her therapy today. She pushed it closed with her leg, grabbed a tea towel and spoon, found the couch, and got comfortable.

Three spoonfuls in, with the room quiet, she opened the door to her thoughts with a key she'd hidden until she was ready.

Donovan had kept her caged with his words and actions—she'd known that for a long time, just as she'd known she wanted away from him. That saying was true; she'd read it the other day while scrolling mindlessly on her phone: **You can't keep dancing with the devil and ask why you're still in hell.**

She took another mouthful, the coldness setting her resolve. This was it. She was separating herself from Donovan Caine. A slight urgency set up shop in her chest now that she'd made an absolute decision. Somehow, she knew if it wasn't now, she would be collateral damage in his war with everyone else and himself. She'd like to think she would have gotten to this place on her own eventually, but knowing Damien and the others were there for her straightened her spine.

And she did have feelings for Damien. She just couldn't fully accept them or explore them until this door to her life was closed. She believed things happened for a reason, whether good or bad, and maybe her gift and the road her life had taken had meant to lead to him, to find Damien Nikolas.

There was a soul-deep connection with him, but she had to close one chapter, end one story, before she could start another. That was just her rule.

Exhaustion hit her. She pushed herself up, putting the lid back on the ice cream, storing it for next time—there was always a next time. Sadie's bed was calling. Tomorrow would be an ending and a beginning. She felt better knowing Damien's friends were outside. When she'd gotten in earlier, her phone had been blown up by missed calls and texts from Donovan. She'd sent one reply: **I'll see you tomorrow at the museum.**

She chose the museum because of safety in numbers—there were always others around. She hoped Donovan would listen to her and let her move on. Rose-colored glasses? Maybe a little.

She turned off the lights as she headed to her bedroom, the soft glow from her solar window charm guiding her to her bedside lamp. Switching it on, her shirt hit the floor first, then her pants. Her gaze caught in her mirror by the emerging colors on her back.

It was breathtaking.

Sadie didn't have any tattoos—she'd never wanted to chance someone touching her that long. But this? She turned her body to see how the serpent dipped to her lower back, then followed her spine and wrapped over her shoulder. A kaleidoscope of hues she couldn't even name, they were so intricate. Her body lit up with thoughts of Damien. Damn, she wanted him here, but she knew she needed to do this on her own.

She slid between the sheets, turned off her light, and hoped sleep would find her. She needed to be sharp tomorrow.

---

*An artillery shell exploded, the sheer power jarring her, yet she couldn't move. Debris catapulted upward, then downward in a wave of an earth shower, crashing upon the soldiers who would forever remain on this hillside for history.*

*Darkness closed in as the last of the day's light dipped, exchanging places with a starry night. Limbless soldiers, their cries echoing around and through her, life shrinking down to the need to move while being paralyzed. Sadie's heart pounded in the cage of her chest, frantic to escape, to run and never look back.*

"I can't," she stammered, trying to pull herself out of this vision as screams of agony formed a vicious chorus around her.

"Sadie, you can. Do you see the gold?" Donovan's voice came to her through a long tunnel.

*Destruction and calamity kept her in a near-petrified stance. A horrific blast from a cannon separated the front of the train from the rear, the back end falling off the tracks into the ravine below.*

*Sheets of flames erupted, and zigzag flames assaulted the doomed crew. The cries of women and the shouts of men tore at her heart.*

"I can't!" she whispered again.

Donovan's hand wound tightly around hers, which was tightly wound around a portion of a recovered gold bar. "You can and you will. You owe me more now than ever, Sadie. Read the damn scene for me. Find out what happened to the gold shipment they were transporting that day, or else."

His rage had started the moment she appeared in her parking stall that morning at the museum. He had been waiting, hidden somewhere. She'd barely slung her purse over her shoulder when his face was in hers. The grab to her arm, then the drag toward his sedan—witnessed by no one. There was literally no one around as her head swiveled, her gaze startled by the emptiness.

"You and I have business, Sadie. Depending on how that goes will determine the rest of the day. Get in." Understanding dawned when she saw Drake open the back door, his face unreadable as usual. What was he, she wondered? Rich leather scent smacked her in the face as she did as expected. The door closed as Donovan filled the space next to her. "Drive." The slow swish of the privacy divider going up, then the movement of his car.

"Donovan, listen, about yesterday…"Just his look cut her off.

"Haven't I been good to you? Haven't I given you everything you've wanted? Hoped for? All I asked for was your loyalty and respect. I thought I had it. So here are the new rules, Sadie. You'll have no contact with Damien Nikolas. You will fight whatever poison he has infected you with. And when the time is right, you will become my wife."

A vacuum sucked everything out of their small space, and panic roared to life inside her. Like a passage of time with all her old traumas resurrected, telling her to hide, escape, run. Her existence minimized down to a backseat, history repeating itself again.

"Why so quiet, ma petite? We're perfect for each other. I should have seen it sooner. Now, for the other reason, I want you to myself."

His touch was rough as he pulled her hand onto his leg, splaying her fingers wide. Coolness was placed on her palm, then her fingers wrapped around it. "Do your job, Sadie." Her face intensified as she was pulled immediately into the gold bar's past.

Thoughts of Bane and how he'd drawn on his inner strength during their shared vision. Sadie tried to find the sliver of light she had seen while watching reels of Bane's life, but she couldn't calm herself enough. Donovan's hijacking had screwed up her plans.

"And if you think Damien can help you? Think again. It pays to know people and witches." His snideness seeped into her. "A cloaking spell doesn't come cheap nowadays, but you? You're worth it, Sadie," he whispered in her ear.

Her brain couldn't compute everything she was demanding of it—the vision, Donovan's threats, her own angst.

A slow-rolling fog moved in to cover the scene, and she was thrown back to the now, to the backseat and the man she never really knew. Her head lifted, knowing what she would find, and she was right. He knew her vision had broken off. Anger chiseled his cheekbones and changed his blue eyes to charcoal. His grip tightened on her, a painful moan slipping past her lips.

"Stop, Donovan, please. You're hurting me. You know I can't control it."

Saying that seemed to make it worse. "I've played too nice with you, Sadie. Maybe it's time you saw the true me." His fingers found her chin, his thumbprint sure to be bruised onto her skin. "Then you'd know not to play games."

With those words, a haze cloaked her, and everything around her spun. She heard a little murmur but couldn't make it out. Her free hand clung to his suit jacket—him, her only lifeline, as her stomach threatened to empty.

Moments later, her feet hit solid ground. Her insides tried to catch up with her outside, which had abruptly stopped. Donovan released her and stepped away. Sadie blinked, trying to settle the spins, taking a breath to realize they were in a warehouse of sorts. He had taken them there, just like that, just like Damien had done.

"Sadie, do you remember Gavin? He used to work for me." Donovan's voice was further away now. She turned to find him walking a large circle around a man taped to a chair. His face was so mangled, one eye almost dislodged from its socket, that she almost threw up.

The ground below where he sat was a pool of blood and urine. She wanted the floor to open up and swallow her—take her away from here.

"This is what happens to those who mess with me. You asked a few weeks ago what happened to Jenna, remember? I caught her stealing from me. Let's just say she won't be doing that again." He raised one of his hands, then slowly clenched his fingers into a fist. Gavin started to choke for air, his body shaking against his bindings. Then, with a sharp downward motion, Donovan brought his arm to his side. Gavin's neck made a loud crack and hung wrongly off his shoulder.

He killed him without touching him. Her mind reeled, and she started to back up. He'd killed Jenna, and who knew who else. "You're a killer." Her body was ready to turn and run, his stone-cold stare gluing her to the spot.

"I'm so much worse than that, Sadie."

She saw it then—his ugliness on full display. Her panic caused her to shake outwardly.

"Is it sinking in, Sadie? I own you. You are mine. And if you're not mine, then you are no one's."

Her scream echoed off the walls, Damien's name distorted amongst her terror.

# Chapter 25

Damien sat with his arms crossed over his wide chest in the obsidian-walled study of his father, half-listening as Tartarus discussed succession. His mind was consumed with thoughts of Sadie: honey-blonde tresses shining under the sun, the pure light of her caramel-colored eyes as laughter escaped her. The mating mark between her shoulder blades beckoned him like a silken string drawing him deeper into their bond. Her stubbornness in refusing to stay under the same roof chafed his protection instincts worse than sandpaper on unprotected skin.

He reminded himself for the hundredth time that she was unfamiliar with their world. Yet the truth remained—they were mated, bound by laws older than human civilization. In their world, the mark she bore was stronger than any marriage certificate. The thought of her being alone, vulnerable, tightened his jaw.

Donovan lingering around the museum compounded the matter. Something about the way the man watched Sadie set off warning bells in Damien's head. That was why he had Levi and Enzo watching her house—a decision she had protested vocally. However, there would be no compromise on anything touching her safety.

"Damien!" The word thundered across the study, shaking the old books on the shelf and pulling him from his thoughts.

He turned to his father, studying the imposing form before him. The ruler of the Underworld seemed tailor-made for the fitted black suit he wore, his silver hair combed back from a face etched with thousands of years of experience. Power rolled off him in waves that sent those lesser than himself shaking with terror.

"Your distraction is evident, son," Tartarus said, his voice softening slightly. "But the Underworld requires—"

"We have been through this a million times," Damien cut in, tightness building between his shoulder blades. "I have a kingdom that needs my rule. I cannot take your place in the Underworld. You have other options. Let's revisit those... soon. I'm needed topside, Father."

Tartarus bridged the space between them, his weathered hand falling upon Damien's shoulder. The touch was hot as hellfire, but it carried a father's love nonetheless. "Whatever the case may be, son, I am here for you. Succession is important, as is the stability of the realms, but so is your happiness."

The words hung between them, thick with the unsaid. Both knew, after all Damien had been through, he at least deserved a chance at happiness.

A nod, and he turned, dissipating to reappear in his home. The scent of Sadie—rich vanilla and underlying hints of the museum's ancient books—lingered in the air, an enticing whisper of her recent presence.

Instantly, his body stirred, coiling like a serpent in heat. If she continued to insist on staying in her own apartment, he might find himself relocating to her. A smile curved his lips at how that would set her on fire. Barely had he framed the thought when his cell phone rang.

Enzo's number lit up the screen. "Tell me, Vamp, how is my girl?"

The vampire's reluctance spoke volumes before he finally responded. "There's a problem, boss."

Chill replaced the warmth in Damien's veins. "What problem?"

"Levi and I followed Sadie to the museum. She parked and ..." The pause in Enzo's voice betrayed his struggle. "We lost her. She disappeared."

Damien's body froze, rage eclipsing the happiness he had just felt. His voice lowered to a deadly hiss. "You lost my mate?"

Malevolent energy gathered around him in response to the fury inside. His mind whirled with one scenario after another, each worse than the last, circling around one name—Donovan.

He tapped into his link with Sadie and was met by a hazy, thick mesh of cobwebs.

Darkness coalesced around him like a mantle, and Damien's eyes blazed with supernatural fire. Cold seeped into the room as his power began to rise. Someone had just stolen something that didn't belong to them. They were about to discover why even his father, the king of the Underworld, showed him respect.

"Hold your position," he spat into the phone. "I'm coming."

The air crackled with energy as Damien prepared to flash to the museum. Whoever had taken Sadie would shortly realize the irrevocable error they'd just made. After all, he was not just a ruler of a kingdom but a mated male.

---

Fury twisted through Damien, contorting, becoming its own entity. Before him stood Enzo and Levi, fighters of inestimable strength, yet he could sense their unease at their failure.

He fought to contain himself. In his head, Enzo and Levi were family, but in those raw moments, the animal inside him salivated for revenge.

Through their mindlink, he growled at his brother, his most trusted friend, Bane. His words cut through the connection like a hot knife. "I need you here now. They lost my mate, mi tesoro. She's been taken, and I can smell a witch responsible for this cloaking spell. I can still scent her in the air. We have to find her quickly, or I will tear this world apart."

Bane's voice came sharp, his Scottish brogue heavier than usual. "Aye, ah'm comin' faster than any wee bat oot o' hell can wing its way, me pal. Keep yer edge sharp, an' ah'll be swoopin' in tae help rip this world tae bloody bits!"

Enzo, being a vampire, could pinpoint a fly flying overhead of a dung heap, while Levi, a Lycan, could track a scent through slabs of concrete and steel. The two looked bedraggled and beaten. Supposedly the best at protecting anyone, they had botched it.

"Find that witch now!" Damien roared, his voice booming into the ground.

In a snap, Enzo disappeared into the night, a blur of motion Levi transformed into his massive Lycan form, blacker than night, his eyes glowing with predatory intensity. They would not fail again.

Dark energy coalesced around Damien. Tendrils of writhing, serpentine appendages of pure force leaped from his skin, each one a living, pulsing weapon, hungry and seeking.

Bane emerged, his huge body radiating menace. "Let's go find that demon bastard and make him pay fer takin' yer mate. We'll show him nae mercy."

Before Damien could respond, Levi was back. A scrawny woman dangled from his monumental jaws, her body limp and broken. He dropped her onto the ground and shifted to human form.

"Sorry, Damien. I'm afraid I pierced her with my fangs," Levi said. "She wouldn't stop talking. I told her this is what happens when one plays with the devil—they get burned."

The energy emanating from Damien intensified. He lifted her, suspending her in the air. Her dark, inky hair swirled around her elongated form like a vortex, arms and legs extended. His serpentine tendrils encircled her, tightening gradually and deliberately.

"I will only ask this once," Damien said, his tone frigid enough to cause harm. "Where is my mate?"

The bravado she carried buckled under his glare. She whispered now, her voice trembling, laced with deep-seated terror. "I had no choice. Donovan said he would take my daughter from me. She is all I have. I know he owns storage facilities in Long Beach, near the Marina. It's his second home.

I'd bet my life he's there. Let me go, and you'll never see me again."

Bane leaned in, his voice thick with menace. "If we ever hear tell o' ye sidin' wi' anyone other than the House o' Nikolas, I'll personally drag ye tae hell myself an' show ye what true pain is, so help me God."

Damien released her, and the witch crashed to the ground, bones shattering from the impact. "We know who you are. You can be found anywhere, at any time. As can those you call friends and family. Get out of my town. Never return. Next time, your life becomes forfeit."

She nodded, whispering her agreement, then turned and scurried into the night.

"Let's go find my mate," Damien ordered.

---

The smell of blood assaulted their nostrils when they finally reached the warehouse. His mating mark seared against his skin—something was wrong. Not just a symbolic mark but an intrinsic part of bonding, sharing emotions from one mate to the other. Damien's hard voice sliced through the dread. "Enzo, Levi! Secure the perimeter. Every inch. No one enters, no one leaves."

Bane moved beside him and whispered, "Sure enough, this is gonnae be a bluid-bath, mark ma words!"

The warehouse door swung wide under the force of Damien's rage. The scent of blood slammed into them as they sped through the building.

In the far back, he found Sadie, pure fear shining in her eyes. Donovan's laughter filled the space—a sound full of malice. "Well, well. Look who finally decided to grace us with their presence."

Power surged within Damien, extended, flexed, and shot from his body, ready to unleash hell itself.

"Let her go," he roared, beyond human comprehension. "OR I WILL DESTROY EVERYTHING YOU ARE."

Donovan kept Sadie plastered to his side, a malevolent smile spreading across his face. Slowly, almost thoughtfully, he reached into his back pocket, pulled out a gun, and jammed the cold barrel against her side. His low-toned words carried a fatal promise. "If I can't have her, nobody will."

The trigger began to squeeze.

Time froze.

Bane growled, "Och, ye might want tae reconsider that choice, ye wee bastard."

Pent-up hostility shook the warehouse, and Damien's energy coiled upward, a raging storm ready to break. Sadie's eyes locked onto Damien's. Their connection transcended the chaos surrounding them.

Everything balanced on a knife's edge.

The gun exploded. Time stood still as he watched his mate's body go limp and fall to the floor. Crimson blood poured from her small frame into a pool around her.

Then the war began.

# Chapter 26

Sadie's heart hammered against her ribs the moment Damien sensed her terror. Their tether ignited in her veins—first with trepidation, then pure rage. That rage amplified her own fear to epic proportions. This was about to go from bad to complete shit.

Damien would find her. She had no doubt. Donovan knew it, too. Without blinking, he materialized beside her, his grip crushing her arm even through her shirt. The hardness of his body pressed against her side, tension radiating from every muscle. She tried to move but felt anchored to the spot.

The air crackled around them. Her monster stood fierce and ready to battle.

Sadie should have known how this day would unfold. A stiff, bitter wind had swept around her when she'd left her place just after first light. The sky had remained that same cold, threatening shade of gray as time ticked by. Now the clouds finally purged themselves, rain hammering the metal roof above. Thunder and lightning accompanied Damien's arrival—even the elements recognized the threat.

It struck her that she'd spent years dodging dangers as a homeless girl on the streets, yet the real danger had been prowling around her for years, masquerading as her safe haven. Donovan had played her, and she'd let him. She'd let him manipulate and coerce her, going along with it all.

Now she stood at a precipice, staring at a future she'd never imagined months ago. But Donovan would never let her go to make a new life with Damien.

Everything funneled down to a spectrum of time—a medieval clock, each hand striking off the seconds. She heard Damien and Bane, heard Donovan, but as if from a great distance. She recognized this sensation of suspension. It was how she entered each vision. She called it the *last sight*—the first thing she felt before being carried elsewhere.

This felt the same but deeper, with a strangulation of forever. Her blood raced in torrents through her heart, desperate to escape.

She'd been fighting her feelings about Damien. He'd met her at a crossroads in her life when her need to be free of Donovan consumed her thoughts—to make her own decisions, to be like she was before she met him, just smarter and more mature. Damien's mark had felt like another cage.

Now all she wanted was to be in his arms.

"Damien—" The word barely escaped before gunfire shattered time. Agony tore through her. She slid downward through Donovan's loosening hold, the cool concrete floor of the warehouse becoming her deathbed. Maybe if she'd ever glimpsed her own future, she'd have run from Donovan sooner.

Wishes never came true, though.

---

Donovan had dismissed the stories as oversized rumors, drunken tales spun by weak men. But his bravado nose-dived when Damien transformed into the most heinous creature he'd ever witnessed. The rumors were true—but not nearly complete enough. He'd fucked up and needed to get the hell out of here.

Unfortunately for Sadie, she knew too much. He couldn't keep her—not with him, not alive.

**Cut your losses**—three words he lived by. He could start over; he'd done it before. After learning what he could from Frankie and Lucas, their executions had been swift, and he'd risen as the new head. No one questioned it. No one raised a mutiny.

He pulled Sadie tighter against him while keeping Damien and his companion in sight. One last kiss to the softness of her hair—her scent always reminded him of sunshine on a beautiful day.

The shot's loudness jarred even him. There wouldn't be another Sadie. Her gift was too rare. A shame, but he'd won. Damien wouldn't have her either.

"It's been fun. Have a nice life, Nikolas." He dropped the gun and attempted to dematerialize, but nothing happened. He couldn't shift.

That's when he saw it barreling toward him—a hound from hell.

---

Damien's monster surged to the surface, a wave of unrestrained misery. The cry that erupted from his lips wasn't noise but concentrated, elemental agony threatening the world's integrity. His mate had been shot. That pathetic piece of shit had hurt the most precious thing to him.

He slammed down beside Sadie, his menacing size more pronounced by shaking fear than rage. It made her seem like a feather in his arms, so fragile compared to the vast scope of his pain. Her pulse whispered against his fingertips, a specter barely supporting her against the void.

"Hold on, mi tesoro," he whispered, his voice breaking. Tears—a sight no one had ever witnessed—were molten fire carving tracks down his face. "Don't you dare die on me. We have a future to fight for. A future I won't let slip away."

His head jerked toward Bane, the infernal dog whose allegiance blazed brighter than the flames consuming the demon's flesh. Donovan hung suspended from Bane's jaws, a humiliated specimen before the devoted animal.

"Take him to Tartarus." Damien's growl was an incantation of raw anger, full of rampant energy's threat. "Make sure he can't escape. I'll deal with that fucker later. Right now, my mate's life is all that matters."

Bane dragged Donovan through the darkest paths between realms. As Damien's oldest and most loyal friend—a hellhound who had stood by the god of monsters through countless battles—his rage burned hotter than his supernatural flames. The bond between Damien and Bane ran deeper than brotherhood, forged in numerous conflicts and shared struggles.

"Ye thought ye could harm me brother's mate, ye miserable piece o' shite?" Bane's voice was more beast than language. "I've seen wars that would make yer soul weep. I've walked through countless hells, and ye think ye can touch what belongs to me best friend?"

He hauled Donovan closer, his body's flames burning so intensely that the air around them warped and twisted. "Tartarus willnae be kind to ye, ye ken? Every moment'll be an eternity o' pure torment. Every bloody breath'll be a desperate prayer for mercy that'll never, EVER come."

---

Damien clutched Sadie to his chest, her breathing shallow and labored. He looked skyward. "Mother!" he thundered, calling to the goddess herself. "I call upon you now! My mate's life hangs in the balance. I beg you—save her!"

The ground bloomed with vines and flowers as the goddess of life knelt beside her son, her hand wiping his tears away. Her heart ached for him. "I'll do whatever it takes to keep her alive, but my son, remember—she'll no longer be human. She'll become immortal like us."

"I can't imagine living without her. Please, Mother, do what you must."

The vision of her son crying jolted memories of him losing his own child, a moment that had brought her to her knees. Damien's sobs struck her dead in the chest, her heart clutching as he'd delivered the most terrifying news any grandparent could hear.

Damien's wife had held their three-month-old son underwater until his body went limp and his soul departed completely. Not even she nor Damien could bring him back. The two most powerful deities had been powerless.

This time, Gaia was here to help her son avoid losing another love. She would do whatever it took to save Sadie—the one true happiness in her son's life, the one who'd brought him from darkness back into light.

Gaia's transformation of Sadie was wonder and terror to behold. Roots of pure emerald light wove through her body, replacing mortality with immortal essence. One vine, then another, then another. As the last vine settled, Gaia's expression softened.

"She will live," the goddess pronounced, "but the change requires rest. She'll sleep deeply until tomorrow. I'll guard her myself. You need to handle the one who did this."

Damien's monster surged inside him, a promise of vengeance. "I'll make him suffer," he whispered, kissing Sadie's forehead before turning to his mother.

Gaia's eyes shone with ancient knowledge. "Go, my son. Your vengeance awaits."

---

The moment Damien entered Tartarus, reality swayed. Shadows coiled around him—a powerful, ancient force of nature. With every step, the ground shook beneath him. Chained and broken, Donovan watched his approach, horror filling his stare, fear so profound it touched every fiber of his being.

Damien's voice was no longer sound but a summoning. "You thought you could touch what's mine?"

His approach was methodical, predatory. With each step, Donovan's chains heated, glowing white-hot. The runes that etched the iron pulsed with unholy light, drawing power directly from Damien's rage.

"You fucking bastard. You shot my mate! She is my universe, my breath, my reason for being."

Damien leaned closer. Donovan could see the monster behind the man—infinite darkness swirling in his eyes, ancient powers older than time itself dancing with murderous intent.

"Your life," Damien whispered, "hangs by a thread thinner than a single hair. I could unmake you. Erase you from every possible timeline. Destroy not just your physical form but your very essence."

The chains around Donovan began constricting, each link pressing into his flesh. Blood seeped and pooled beneath him.

Bane watched from the sidelines, his colossal hellhound form perfectly still, dark flames licking around his obsidian fur. His eyes gleamed with predatory satisfaction, knowing his best friend was about to deliver judgment more terrifying than any punishment Tartarus could devise.

"You fucked up," Damien said, every word a sentence of doom. "Now you'll understand what suffering truly is."

---

**Mi tesoro** whispered from somewhere far away. She tried to grasp those words, but she couldn't move, couldn't hold on. She was slipping under and away from the man she loved, her body consumed by agony.

Was she in a vision? Sadie spun through endless, miserable loops. Tendrils snaked around her legs and slithered up her body, pulling her deeper into a black hole. She tried to lift her arms, but they became entangled in rope-like strands, her efforts useless.

The whimpering she heard was her own. Her eyelids felt heavy, sealed shut, refusing to open. This was the end. She couldn't fight anymore—her fight was gone. Donovan had won again.

---

An illumination somewhere distant disturbed her slumber. Was she sleeping? She felt cocooned, warm. Her eyelids still felt heavy, yet she thought she saw... something.

Images, blurry at first like a movie reel, sped by, then slowed. A pale crescent moon slipped in and out of view behind deathly ominous clouds, the smell of rain threatening. She could hear leaves rustling, feel the wind's coolness, taste the musty odor of spoiled food hanging thick in the air. This felt familiar—it sparked a memory.

Her first night on the streets hadn't been what she'd imagined. Sadie had thought she was prepared, but she wasn't. Leers and strange looks from others had set her panic meter too high. Finding a secluded place to hide and sleep, never closing her eyes once, living every minute in fight-or-flight mode. Why now? Why this memory?

Then another. Morbid dread snaked down her spine as she saw the lifeless body of that young girl, no older than herself, the one she'd spoken to the day before. They'd looked so much alike: long blonde hair, denim jeans, knapsacks holding their worldly possessions. But now her lifeless eyes stared skyward, the area roped off while police officers sipped coffee from styrofoam cups, as if she weren't dead on the dirty concrete beside them. Sadie's thought: *That could have been me.*

Then another. His watch—a Rolex peeking through as his jacket cuff shifted. She'd never seen Donovan without it, no matter what he wore. It was always on his wrist, somehow threatening maybe because it was tied to the man, present for every unlawful, horrific thing he'd ever done.

And then another glimpse: emerald shadings, smoky lines, and the eye of a serpent. Damien's mark. Her heart beat faster with purpose, her body stirred with desire, and whatever weight had been holding her down shattered around her.

A deep inhale brought fresh breath into her lungs. Her lashes fluttered open, her eyes witnessing flourishes of color she'd never seen before. And a woman she'd never encountered.

"Where am I? Where's Damien?"

"My son will be along shortly, Sadie. Do you feel like you could sit up? Would you like some tea? I have a special blend that will clear the last of your cobwebs."

"Tea?" Her own voice sounded different. Maybe she wasn't really here, wherever here was. Maybe she was hallucinating.

Pushing herself up slightly, she couldn't wait. She needed to know. Her hand reached out, touching the other woman's. Her vision was instant and more full of color and life than any had ever been—like she'd upgraded to the deluxe package. Every sensory perception was heightened. As images of the woman's life assaulted her, pieces snapped into place one after another. Sadie pulled her hand back, clasping it within the other.

"Oh my god."

"I am one, yes, Sadie. As is my son, your mate. Now, how about that tea? Then you can tell me what you just did."

# Chapter 27

Damien released his monster slowly. Serpents crawled down his arms, hissing with malevolent hunger. A sinister grin pulled at the corners of his lips as Donovan's eyes widened. Behind the chained demon, Bane's laughter echoed through the chamber.

"The pain ye're aboot tae experience is just the start, lad," Bane whispered, his voice like grinding stone. "Every day that passes will bring a new level of agony, an' ye'll be beggin' fer death, but that wee blessing will ne'er come yer way. Death is a luxury ye don't deserve, ye ken?"

The god of monsters loomed over Donovan, each deliberate step echoing through the chamber like a death knell. Serpents slithered outward from Damien—dark as midnight, scales gleaming with malice. They rasped against the stone floor as they encircled their prey.

"You can't break me, asshole," Donovan whispered, barely audible.

Damien chuckled, the sound devoid of warmth. "You want to fucking bet? Watch and learn, demon."

His words cut short as the first snake wrapped around Donovan's ankle. Its bite struck cold as steel and ice, followed by more serpents weaving through the links of his chains, slowly constricting. The metallic rattling of his restraints filled the air as he struggled in desperation. Each movement seemed to invite the snakes closer.

Damien watched with cold satisfaction as his serpents tightened their hold, forked tongues flicking out to taste their victim's fear. Their jaws unhinged, revealing rows of curved fangs that gleamed in the dim light.

Layer upon layer of snakes covered and entwined Donovan's flesh. A guttural roar of anguish echoed off the chamber walls as liquid fire coursed through his veins. With each heartbeat, the poison spread deeper through his shaking body.

Damien stepped closer, golden eyes ablaze with ancient fury. "You thought to take her from me?" His tone carried the weight of mountains, the rage of storms.

The serpents wound tighter, slick with Donovan's blood. New fangs tore fresh skin as Damien's pets struck repeatedly, delivering more venom with each bite to his vital points.

"Fuck you!" Donovan wheezed between electric jolts of agony.

"Silence!" Damien roared. Dust shook loose from the ceiling. "You played with the wrong god, little man. You thought there wouldn't be consequences?" He dropped to his haunches, face inches from Donovan's contorted features. "Now you'll reap what you've sown. My darlings will make your death endless, and I'll savor every second of your torment."

Bane in his hellhound form, eyes like burning coals reflecting wars of ages past. "Make him suffer," Damien commanded, voice cold as winter frost. "But keep him alive. He'll feel pain for the rest of his fucking existence."

Bane's muzzle drew back in a terrible grin, revealing teeth forged in hellfire. The hound took humanoid form, wrapping burning fingers around Donovan's throat. Screams mingled with satisfied serpent hisses as flames licked across skin.

Damien wrapped shadows around himself. Space buckled to his will, and instantly he materialized in his mother's villa in Palermo, Sicily. Ancient stone walls thrummed with centuries of accumulated power.

Gaia waited in the corridor, emerald robes flowing like mist. "My son," she said, eyes reflecting the weight of millennia. "She's awake." Something—hidden meaning—flickered across her timeless features. "There's more you should know, but first..." She gestured toward her bedchamber. "Go to her."

---

As Damien approached the elaborate doors where Sadie waited, his heart thundered. He entered Gaia's bedchamber—a sanctuary of soft lamplight and dancing shadows. Ancient tapestries draped the walls, and the air hung thick with healing herbs and magic.

Sadie sat on the edge of a great four-poster bed, her blonde hair now shot through with shining silver threads. A subtle glow of immortality radiated from her skin. She looked up—eyes still the warm brown that had first captured his heart, now sparked with divine gold.

In an instant, Damien was beside her, drawing her into his arms. "I thought I'd lost you. I begged my mother to do whatever it took to keep you alive."

She pulled him closer, lips finding his. The kiss deepened with all the longing of separation and joy of reunion. Above them, divine energy crackled like lightning across the midnight sky as their powers blended as seamlessly as their bodies.

"I need you," she breathed against his mouth. "Now. I need you now."

Their clothes fell away like autumn leaves, forgotten on the floor. He laid her back against silken sheets, hovering above her in adoration. "You're even more beautiful," he breathed, trailing his mouth along her neck. "My goddess. My mi tesoro."

Sadie arched into his touch, fingers tracing his chest's contours, mapping every inch as if to convince herself this wasn't another dream. "I love you," she gasped as their bodies finally joined. "I'll always find my way back to you."

Their energy electrified the room as they moved together, shadows dancing on the walls. The air hummed with divine electricity. Every touch was fire, every kiss a promise of forever. They lost themselves in each other repeatedly.

He worshiped her body as if she were the goddess she'd become; Sadie matched his passion. They were opposing forces of nature finding balance—darkness and light, two pieces of the same soul, finally whole.

Dawn's first pink light colored the sky as they lay tangled and breathless. Sadie traced lazy circles on Damien's chest while he ran fingers through her disheveled hair.

"Promise me," she whispered against his skin. "Promise we'll never be torn apart again."

He tightened his hold, pressing his lips to her forehead. "By every realm and every ounce of power within me, nothing will ever come between us again. You're mine through all eternity, as I am yours."

Morning light danced across the golden flecks in her eyes as she smiled up at him. Damien's heart swelled with love so intense it bordered on pain. Together, they had transcended mortality—their bond strengthened by transformation.

Lying there, savoring their reunion, neither noticed the knowing glance in Gaia's eyes as she passed the bedroom door, her secret held close—for now.

---

In Tartarus's lowest circle, where even ancient demons feared to tread, Bane commanded every pathway. His massive form rippled between realities—a hellhound large as a small house, fur of woven void matter that consumed light, eyes blazing with creation's first fire. Tartarus itself shook at his approach, recognizing power that predated even this realm of eternal torment.

Donovan hung in chains forged from chaos metal—only that could hold such a demon. His true form was partially revealed: obsidian skin cracked with molten lava veins, wings of shattered glass trailing streams of blood-red energy. Yet even that mighty demonic form trembled beneath Bane's advance.

Bane's voice echoed through multiple dimensions as he circled his prey. "Och, demon flesh regenerates sae much faster than mortal meat. Makes it perfect fer gettin' creative, ye ken?" His form shifted into something ancient and terrible that had existed before shape and form were fully conceived.

Donovan sneered, but sulfur eyes flickered with fear. "Do your worst, dog. I've endured all measures of—" His bravado shattered into screams as Bane's power struck.

This wasn't hellfire—this was primal flame, the fire that shaped the first realms. It burned demon flesh to cinder, seared through magical protections, and charred the very essence of Donovan's immortal soul. Other hellhounds could burn the physical, but Bane's flames devoured memory and hope—the fabric of being itself.

"Ye've mistaken somethin' fundamental," Bane growled voice rumbling like colliding galaxies. "I'm nae common hellhound. I was the First. I strode beside primordials when the universe was young, when reality hadn't yet congealed into concrete fact." His crystallized shadow claws tore across Donovan's demonic form, rending not flesh and tissue but the magical matter composing supernatural existence.

"And ye," he continued, voice dropping to a terrible rumble as he shifted to humanoid form—a towering figure of void and flame, "ye dared harm the one being I've chosen as friend. The god who saw me as equal, not a weapon."

Bane placed a hand against Donovan's chest and began pulling—not at flesh or bone, but something deeper. The demon's fundamental essence. Donovan screamed as his very being was slowly torn from itself.

"The problem wi' being a demon," Bane mused as he worked, "is that ye cannae truly die. Which means I can tear ye apart on levels most beings cannae comprehend, and ye'll always reform. Always heal. Always be ready fer our next... session."

Minutes stretched into hours, seeming like eternities, as Bane demonstrated his full power. He tore apart Donovan's demonic form layer by layer, scorched away supernatural energies, and employed powers that predated torture itself. Screams echoed through Tartarus that would have driven lesser beings mad.

When the session ended, Bane returned to hellhound form, each departing step leaving cracked, burning reality in its wake. "I'll see ye tomorrow, demon," he growled. "And the next day. And every day until the stars burn out and reality crumbles. Ye cannae escape our appointments. Best get used tae our wee chats, aye?"

# Chapter 28

Sadie woke first. Lying on her side, Damien wrapped around her, her lashes slowly lifting to the low light peeking through the hanging drapery over the window on the far side of the room. To say her mind and body felt out of sorts was mild. She felt more herself, though at this moment, than yesterday, while she sat sharing a cup of tea with Damien's mother.

Nothing like getting a crash course of gods and goddesses, and realizing your in-laws, if she could even call them that, were basically around since the beginning of time. She hadn't seen Damien's father yet, but Gaia had told her he ruled in the underworld. So how that worked, she wasn't sure, but … baby steps.

All Sadie knew right now was that she was made up of new wiring. Her human life was over; she was now immortal because of Gaia's powers and Damien's mark. What that all meant and how it worked, she'd learn; Gaia said she'd help in any way.

Sadie could tell how much Damien's mother loved him, and it tore at her own heart. She'd never known that in her life. One thing she knew without a doubt, if she ever had children, they would know love, hugs, and safety.

"What's wrong?" Damien's arms tightening around her. The warm stroke of his breath against her cheek.

A soft smile played along her lips. "Why do you think something's wrong? Maybe everything is finally just right."

His lips brushed along the spot just below her ear. "I felt deep sorrow through our connection. It will always be the way now and forever."

Forever had a whole different meaning now that she was …immortal; trying that out again in her head.

Turning herself, so she laid on her back, staring up into the face of her … mate; trying that word out too because she was finding new courage on her new path, something dawning on her at that moment. "Will I have special abilities now, too, or will my gift change in any way?" Another angst moment, wondering if the anxiety that could derive from her visions would be intensified.

His hand cupping her cheek, his gaze searching within hers. "Sadie, we'll find out together how your transformation has affected you. But I'm here, and so is my family and our friends. You have a very protective circle around you now. We'll figure it all out. I promise."

Damien could sense every emotion flowing through her, a vulnerability that made the mated male in him rise and know that nothing would harm her again.

"I have something for you. There's no bow or box, but it comes from my heart. It comes from a place that up until I met you, has been buried and unreachable." His deep timber burrowing underneath her skin, a warmth flowing like firelight on a chilly night. And Sadie realized his emotions were running through her. Their connection, alive and deeper than before.

"Damien, there's nothing I need. I have you and that's all I'll ever want…." Sadie was about to say more, but his kiss stopped her. A shutter of pleasure raced down her spine, but before she could pull herself closer, he lifted those sexy lips off of hers.

"I want you to touch me with your hands. I have something to share with you. But before you do, I have to tell you it's heartbreaking. It's where my heart broke before you mended it."

And Sadie knew what she would see.  Bane and Kimora had told her about his devastating loss.

Pressing herself tighter against him. "I've touched you before, and never once have I seen anything. And I know about your son. I don't want you to relive that again."

"Sadie. You haven't read me because I wouldn't allow it. I'm the god of monsters; my powers are endless. But I need to do this, for myself and for us. There will be no walls between us or secrets. You're my forever; she never was. But my son was everything and her hate of me ended his life. It's horrific, but there are other pieces of great joy and love. I want to show you. Will you let me?"

Her monster was a sweet, loving man. His own uncertainty and unrestrained emotions washed through her, and she knew he needed this. For himself as well as them.

She lifted herself slightly, her lips finding his before separating. "Ok. Remind me later to start something about the whole blocking me thing though…" trying to lighten the mood before the past rose up.

His devilish grin, the one she'd always known since day one was going to be trouble, beamed down at her. "I'm going to keep you too busy to argue." Her body heating at his words.

"I love you." Those words were out before Sadie even thought of them. How he changed her life in a short few months was a true miracle. "Are you ready?" And she didn't want to move or shift how they were at this moment. This was just them, intimate, secluded, in their own bubble.

His nod and she raised her hands gently, one cupping around his neck and the other around his cheek, pulling his forehead down to hers.

A door burst open to his past, drawing gasps from each of them. Sadie didn't know if it was because of their mating or her new powers, but the vision was acute, more vivid. Reels of Damien's life superimposing one after the other. Some snippets so short, she just caught a glimpse, and others, she realized, the ones that scarred and damaged him, slowed down. The rawness and pain was more than she thought she could bear, but she drew it out of him into her, not knowing how she could, she'd never done that before. But for him, she would do anything.

Moments turned to minutes, turned to… she didn't know. All she knew was she held on, holding them together until the final scene. Until the purge was over, and they grabbed each other tighter, murmuring soft words, light caresses turning to harsher touches. Surrendering herself to every and each exquisite sensation. Instinct, driving them both, nothing else mattering, except the joining of their bodies, becoming one.

"Ti amo lu me tesoro." his accent, heavy and thick against her lips.

And the first tear slipped from her eyes, caught by his mouth and then more followed because his love filled every nuance of her body. She didn't doubt his words; she felt everyone. All the little hiding places that were inaccessible to others and even herself were now filled with life.

"Don't cry, Sadie."

"They're happy tears, baby. They're happy tears."

…

Damien felt an overwhelming wave of happiness wash over him, like a gentle tide caressing the shore, as he cradled Sadie in his arms once more. The warmth of her presence enveloped him, wrapping around him like a soft, comforting blanket, shielding him from the world's chill. In that precious moment, the thought of a life without her seemed impossible, as if she were the essence that gave his existence meaning and purpose. Her laughter danced through the air like rays of sunlight breaking through a dense canopy of clouds, chasing away every shadow that dared to linger in the recesses of his mind and illuminating his world with a vivid, radiant glow that he had long thought unattainable.

Together, they would forge a tapestry of countless adventures, each memory glistening like brilliant jewels threaded into the fabric of their relationship. Moments filled with laughter, joy, and even the occasional tear had woven deeper connections between their souls, creating an unbreakable bond that transcended the ordinary.

Sadie had done more than fill his life with joy and laughter; she had gently pieced together the shattered fragments of his heart, which past struggles and heartache had long fragmented. Her love had become a lifeline, rescuing him in ways he had never envisioned, transforming his solitary existence into one brimming with vibrant life and renewed hope.

As they sat across from his mother, a palpable sense of anticipation filled the air, thick and electric. Damien, resolved to share the truth about his powers and the immortality that colored his life, he could feel his heart racing with both excitement and apprehension. He hoped that this revelation would cast light on his reality for her, illuminating the experiences he had endured. More importantly, he yearned for her to feel the deep fullness of his love and the unwavering assurance that from that day forward, she would never again have to endure the sting of loneliness.

Gaia, watching her son, felt her heart swelling with pride and joy. A gentle smile blossomed across her face as she observed the radiant light emanating from him, a brilliant reflection of the happiness that Sadie had infused into his life. It was a sight that filled her with an indescribable sense of peace; he was finally whole again. Gaia held a steadfast certainty that he would go to great lengths to protect and cherish her. She had witnessed the darkness that had clouded his heart before, and seeing him now bathed in the warmth of true love was a dream come true.

"Sadie, I want to express my heartfelt gratitude for healing my son and showing him what true love feels like," Gaia said, her voice warm and sincere, brimming with maternal affection.

"Your son has shown me how to love, revealing that I don't need to journey through life alone," Sadie replied, sparkling with sincerity, her eyes glistening with emotion.

Taking Sadie's hand in his, Damien felt a surge of joy ripple through him, causing a broad grin to spread across his face. The warmth of their connection radiated not just between them but enveloped the whole room. "Lu me tesoro, I want to ask you something that aligns with the depths of my heart. You've lived a human life, and I know this world is new to you, even though we are mated, which is akin to a marriage in our kind. I want to give you everything you've ever dreamed of, to build a future together that glimmers with the promise of everlasting love."

With a flourish, he reached into his pocket, pulling out a captivating green emerald ring that seemed to capture the very essence of their love. Its vibrant hue symbolized their unshakeable bond, signifying his mating mark and the life they would build together. He had never experienced such profound feelings before; Damien was undeniably and wholeheartedly in love with her.

"Will you marry me?" he asked, his voice steady yet filled with hopeful anticipation.

Sadie gasped as she peered at the ring, her heart racing. It was perfect—the embodiment of their union and shared dreams. Her heart belonged to him; they might be moving fast, but in their world, this was the next step to take, a promise of a life intertwined.

"Yes, I'll marry you," her voice filled with certainty and joy, the answer spilling forth like a rush of water breaking through a dam.

Gaia sank into her seat, overwhelmed by a warm flood of emotion that spread through her like sunlight breaking through clouds on a cool day. Her son had finally discovered his true mate, and the joy swelling in her heart felt almost too immense to contain. The thought of seeing him so happy, so complete, filled her spirit with a lightness that had long been absent. She could hardly remember a time when she felt such pure elation; it was a poignant reminder of all the trials he had endured. After everything—especially the heartbreak of losing a child—he truly deserved this happiness. No parent should ever have to bear such a devastating loss, and the thought of him finally finding love made her spirit soar.

"It looks like we're going to get your father to crawl out of the underworld after all. Sadie? You haven't met Damien's father and the other half of my soul. But he'll adore you like I do. Our mating is unconventional, but we make it work. Our responsibilities must come before we do. That's the price he and I must pay as rulers and guardians. He is going to be overjoyed with this union."

In that moment, as they basked in the joy of the proposal, time seemed to stand still. The air around them shimmered with possibility, each heartbeat echoing the promise of forever they were ready to embrace. It was not just a union of two souls, but a reclamation of hope, love, and the warmth of shared dreams that lay ahead. They could face whatever challenges life might throw at them together, fortified by their love and the unwavering support of those around them.

# Chapter 29

Damien watched her from across the garden—his immortal bride. The Sicilian sun caught in Sadie's hair, igniting it with copper fire as his mother, Gaia, fussed over her in soothing, gentle tones. Even now, weeks after he'd nearly lost her, his eyes tracked the rise and fall of her chest. A habit carved deep during those agonizing hours when her life slipped away on cold concrete.

Donovan. The name curdled in his mouth like sour wine. Now the bastard rotted in Tartarus, his screams echoing through the depths—a symphony for the damned. Damien's wrath would follow him through eternity.

But today, those dark thoughts could wait. Today was for celebration, for life reborn. For Sadie.

"Ye're brooding again." Bane's massive frame cast a shadow across the flagstones as he approached. Despite his intimidating presence, mischief danced in his ancient eyes.

"Just thinking," Damien replied, his mouth quirking upward.

"Thinkin' o' turnin' that demon inside out again?" Bane's laughter rumbled like Highland thunder. "Kimora's told ye to let it go. What's done is done. She lives."

Damien's gaze drifted back to Sadie. Gaia's hands rested on her shoulders, guiding her through the delicate art of channeling immortal power. His mother had arrived like a force of nature when the bullet found its mark, her hands blazing with creation's fire as she remade Sadie's dying flesh into something eternal. The debt could never be repaid.

"She's adapting well," Bane observed.

"This was always her path," Damien said, conviction threading through his voice. "The mortal shell was just a cocoon. This..." He gestured toward the garden, toward his mother's villa nestled in the Sicilian hills, toward the immortal world that now embraced Sadie, "This was always her destiny."

The garden itself seemed to recognize her presence. Flowers turned toward her as if she were a second sun. Gaia's realm bloomed in impossible beauty—crimson poppies tangled with midnight delphiniums, alabaster lilies reaching toward grass so emerald it seared the eyes. Wisteria cascaded over weathered stone arches, purple blossoms releasing perfume that mingled with the Mediterranean's salt-kissed breeze.

Few mortals had ever witnessed Sicily like this—when gods walked openly and Gaia's power pulsed unchecked through the fertile earth.

"Have ye told her yet, laddie?" Bane's question shattered Damien's reverie.

"Told her what?"

"What it truly means to be yer bride. To be bound to the God of Monsters for eternity."

Damien's jaw tightened. "There's time."

"Less than ye think." Bane nodded toward the garden's eastern edge, where Levi and his wife huddled in intense conversation with Enzo. The ancient vampire's usually composed features betrayed unusual tension as he gestured with precise movements. "Enzo takes his role as father of the bride seriously. He's been practicing his walk for three days."

Despite everything, Damien chuckled. Enzo—who'd watched empires crumble and civilizations rise from ash—rehearsing his steps like a nervous father. "He'll manage."

"And what about ye? How fare the nerves of the God o: Monsters on his wedding eve?"

The question struck deeper than Damien expected. Fear was a luxury he rarely indulged.

"I almost lost her, Bane." The words scraped his throat raw "Nothing else matters after that."

Bane's weathered face softened with understanding. He'd been there in those desperate moments, his rage echoing Damien's own as Sadie's blood pooled beneath them. He'd witnessed Gaia's arrival—a whirlwind of ancient power, her hands blazing with the light of creation itself.

"Kimora's been helping with preparations," Bane continued shifting to safer ground. "She and yer mother have woven protection spells into every flower, every stone."

"No chances," Damien growled.

"None," Bane confirmed.

Movement caught Damien's eye. Sadie had spotted him across the garden, her face transforming with a smile that could have melted winter itself. Love radiated from her newly eternal heart as she excused herself from Gaia and glided toward him, still adjusting to the grace that now flowed through her movements.

"There you are," she said, capturing his hands in hers. "Your mother's been teaching me to coax flowers open with my mind. Watch." She extended her fingers toward a tightly furled rosebud. Slowly, the petals unfurled like silk ribbons, revealing a heart of deepest crimson.

"Incredible," Damien breathed, pride warming his chest.

"Give her time, and she'll be moving mountains," Gaia declared as she joined them, laughter sparkling in her ageless eyes. She looked as she always had—eternal, with skin the rich brown of fertile earth and hair crowned with living vines and blooms. "My son chose wisely."

Heat bloomed across Sadie's cheeks. "I have so much to learn."

"Eternity to learn it," Gaia corrected, her voice gentle as spring rain. "Speaking of which, we still have wedding preparations to finish. Binding two immortal souls requires... careful attention."

"Nothing worthwhile ever comes easy," Damien said, his fingers tightening around Sadie's.

Gaia's gaze pierced straight to his soul. "True. And you, my son, have earned this joy. After millennia of walking alone, you've found your equal." She turned to Sadie, her expression softening. "And you, daughter of my heart, have survived trials that would shatter lesser spirits. Together, you'll be unstoppable."

Damien drew Sadie closer, breathing in her transformed scent. No longer purely human, but now layered with notes of ambrosia and starlight—evidence of his mother's miraculous work.

"Tomorrow," Sadie whispered against his chest.

"Tomorrow," he promised. "Under the Sicilian sun, before those who've stood with us, we'll bind our souls forever."

As the sun descended behind Mount Etna, painting the garden in molten gold, something shifted in Damien's chest. For the first time in his immortal existence, he faced the future with something other than grim determination. With Sadie beside him, eternity stretched ahead not as a burden, but as a gift.

Damien, God of Monsters, had discovered something he'd never dared hope for—a reason to look forward to forever.

# Chapter 30

Sadie twisted her hand in the morning light, watching sunbeams fracture through the emerald on her finger into brilliant shards that blurred her vision. Damien could've slipped a ring from a cereal box onto her finger, and she'd still be a trembling mess. Because it came wrapped in his love and devotion.

Her wedding day. Electric currents fired through her veins, every nerve ending alive with anticipation. She didn't need the ceremony—she and Damien were already bound by love and his sacred mark that now bloomed across her back and shoulder like living art. The most breathtaking thing she'd ever seen. Her secret hope whispered that somehow, she could mark him in return. She wasn't sure how, but she'd find a way.

But Damien wanted this—a ceremony with their friends and his parents present. Something small and intimate. Something for her to treasure. Through their bond, she felt how much this meant to him. Her remarkable male, who'd survived devastating loss yet still opened his heart and made hers a home there. She'd stand before the people who mattered to him and declare her love, not just to their friend and son, but to their god and ruler.

A knock rattled her bedroom door.

"Come in unless you're Damien. Then you wait." Kimora's throaty laugh vibrated through the wood.

"Just letting you know everyone's ready. How are you holding up?"

Sadie had been practicing daily with her emerging powers. Even Gaia hadn't known what abilities would manifest from her healing infusion.

With focused thought—though it required far more concentration than those words implied—she turned the knob and swung the door open from across the room.

"Sweet gods, Sadie, you're stunning. He's going to growl at the sight of you."

"Don't make me tear up, Kimora. This mascara claims to be waterproof, but I'm not testing it." Sadie pulled her into a fierce hug.

Their friendship had deepened over recent weeks. Sadie was still navigating this newness—the reality of having a true family, people to lean on and confide in. Kimora felt like the sister she'd never had. All this happiness in her life, ironically, resulting from Donovan's attempt to destroy it.

She'd asked Damien about Donovan once. His only response: "He's gone, Sadie. He can never hurt you again." She'd left it there, trusting him with her life.

Kimora circled her with predatory grace, taking in the cornflower blue dress Sadie had chosen. "Damien's going to scoop you up and disappear. You might not survive your own vows."

The dress defied tradition—simple elegance in soft satin. Sleeveless, with a neckline that dipped just past her breasts, held by delicate straps. The full-length gown kissed her ankles with understated grace. But the back bordered on scandalous—completely open to just above her lower back dimples, her mating mark on full display. The serpent's emerald eyes seemed to pierce anyone whose gaze fell upon the intricate artwork, a partial train flowing behind her.

"He won't see the back until it's over. That's my plan anyway."

"The gasps as you walk past everyone will ruin that plan. But I'll help where I can."

"Then you're in trouble too, Kimora, because you look like you stepped off a magazine cover."

Kimora was an Egyptian goddess incarnate. Her gold sheath clung like molten metal, ebony hair swept into a high ponytail secured by an exquisite clasp. Matching jewelry adorned her wrists and upper arms—authentic pieces from her birth millennia ago.

When did this become her life? Awe still struck her breathless.

"I'm ready. Let's do this before Damien decides to burst in here, because we both know his patience has limits." Truth rang in her words. If doubt crept in, he'd steamroll through everyone and everything.

"See you out there." Kimora departed, leaving Sadic a moment to collect herself.

Her reflection stared back from the mirror—composed, radiant, ready. She met her own gaze. "You found your forever,

Sadie girl." Moisture threatened, and she blinked hard before heading out the door and down the hall.

---

Was there anything as beautiful as a Sicilian sunset? Yes. Him, standing at the cobbled path's end with the azure sea as his backdrop, surrounded by Gaia's lush garden sanctuary.

Sadie paused, her gaze touching everyone sharing this moment with them. Slight intimidation crept in at the sight of what must be Damien's father standing beside Gaia, but then she found her mate's stare, and her breath simply vanished.

One step, then another. Enzo kept her from bolting down the path. Low murmurs followed their progress. Damien's blue eyes shifted to the others, then locked back on hers.

His father's deep grunt of approval rang over the soft music drifting on the breeze. "She wears our mark well. I approve."

A sharp elbow from Gaia silenced him with a stern "Hush."

"Sadie?" Damien's utter confusion painted his features adorably. Enzo's deep chuckle accompanied his step aside.

"Marry me first. Then I'll show you."

---

Joy crashed over Damien in waves, a grin splitting his face wide. Today, he would marry his soul's other half, the person he'd dreamed of finding but never dared hope existed. Never had he imagined allowing himself such deep love, yet the moment he'd seen her, he'd known—she was his forever, the missing piece finally discovered.

Bane's hand clasped his shoulder, his friend's smile bright enough to illuminate the entire garden. Finally, after a lifetime carved by heartache, Damien was getting everything he deserved. Bane had stood by him through relentless storms, especially when tragedy struck and claimed their sweet boy too soon. Pain had carved deep trenches in Damien's heart, walls rising like fortress stones. But Bane understood—he'd felt that loss too, and witnessing Damien's transformation filled him with hope.

"I've watched ye go through hell and back, my friend," Bane said, emotion thickening his voice. "But now ye're getting what ye deserve. Just remember—yer heart's safe with Sadie. She'll treasure it like the most precious thing in the world."

Damien adjusted his emerald dress shirt, tailored to perfection, the fabric shimmering like fresh leaves in sunlight. His black dress pants provided grounding on this monumental day. "How do I look?"

"Like a man on a mission, Damien. Let's get ye hitched, shall we? This day's all about ye two, and it's bloody grand!" Bane's eyes twinkled with genuine joy.

Everything looked perfect. The sea sparkled under golden light, waves lapping the shore like whispered encouragement. His mother's garden bloomed with lavender and poppies, their sweet fragrance dancing on the breeze. Each petal reflected the love and hope filling his heart. It felt surreal—a beautiful dream he never wanted to end.

Damien's heart thundered as Sadie approached, the world fading away. She embodied every dream—a radiant vision in flowing cornflower blue that cascaded around her like a spilled sky. The fabric caught the breeze, making her appear to glide rather than walk, each step a heartbeat pulling him closer to forever.

His breath caught. For a moment, he froze, completely captivated. The gentle curve of her smile, the way sunlight crowned her hair—she looked like the angel he'd envisioned but never believed he'd find. Longing and love swelled within him, a tidal wave of emotion that nearly brought him to his knees.

Moisture threatened his eyes as he drank in the sight. This woman had become his soul's missing piece, bringing light back after darkness had claimed so much. In her dress, like a field of cornflowers reaching for the sun, he saw hope, warmth, and an unbreakable bond that would carry them through whatever life threw their way.

Sadie was his heart, and he would protect her with everything he possessed. A silent promise whispered through him—this was their moment, their love story that would shine brighter than any darkness they'd faced.

When she reached him, their eyes locked, and the world melted away entirely. Nothing mattered except her. "You look breathtaking," he managed, voice thick with emotion. Her smile confirmed what he already knew—he was the luckiest man alive.

Tartarus clasped his son's shoulder. "Let's get on with the ceremony so you can get to the best part—the honeymoon." His chuckle carried warmth that eased Damien's nerves while stoking his anticipation.

"Husband, there will be plenty of time for that. Now step back and let our son marry his mate." Gaia moved to the makeshift altar, the goddess of rebirth honoring them as officiant.

As the ceremony commenced, gentle wave sounds harmonized with rustling leaves overhead. Guests gathered, faces turned toward the radiant couple, hearts brimming with happiness. Sunlight danced, creating a golden halo around Sadie, enhancing her ethereal beauty. The universe seemed to conspire in blessing this union, making anything feel possible.

"My son has found love. His true love. The one he was meant to find when she was meant to be found. Love finds us when we're ready to receive it—a vine of eternity weaving through the abyss, pulling two hearts together. And here we are." Gaia took one hand from each of them. "We are all here as your family to say we stand with you and beside you. Sadie, you hold my son's heart, and Damien, you keep her soul. This is only the beginning, my children."

When the time came for vows, Damien stood before Sadie, his heart swelling with emotions that struggled to find words. He drew a deep breath, focusing on her—the light of his life, his beacon through the darkest storms.

"Sadie, my divine goddess," he began, voice steady yet passionate, "before time began, I ruled shadows and commanded night, but my realm felt incomplete until your light found me. As the God of Monsters, I have commanded legions; today, however, I surrender my immortal heart to you alone. I vow to stand beside you through eternal nights and endless days, cherishing your divinity as it complements my darkness. When worlds collapse and new ones form, my love for you will remain constant in all creation. You are my balance, my strength, my salvation. In your eyes, even my monsters find beauty. In your touch, even my darkness discovers peace. For all eternity, my power and protection are yours. I promise to nurture your dreams, honor your spirit, and share every joy and sorrow as we walk this path together. With you, shadows feel less daunting, and light shines brighter. I pledge to lift you when you need it most and honor you daily with the love and respect you deserve.

Today, surrounded by our loved ones, I bind my fate to yours, forever and always."

Magic shimmered in the atmosphere as his vows ended, love enveloping them like a warm embrace. Sadie stepped closer to share her vows, Damien's heart racing with every beat, knowing their journey together was just beginning.

"Damien," her fingers entwined with his as she moved closer. "You're stubborn, arrogant, and sexy as hell. You're trouble with the biggest capital T. But most of all, you're mine for eternity. I promise to be your sanctuary and your anchor. I'm standing here in love with the monster of my dreams, wearing his mark on my body and heart. It was always you, even before I knew it was you."

After speaking her heartfelt vows, Sadie turned gracefully, allowing Damien to appreciate her dress's exquisite back fully. The fabric cascaded down, elegantly cut low just above her hips, creating a striking silhouette that accentuated her figure.

...

He was stunned and captivated by the sight of her mating mark. The serpent had transformed from a modest imprint into stunning artwork. Starting at her shoulder's nape, it wove beautifully across her skin, scales appearing almost luminescent. It coiled and slithered down her back, sinuous and graceful, before tapering elegantly to her right hip's curve. The way it melded with her skin and dress's delicate fabric gave her an ethereal quality—a perfect blend of beauty and otherworldliness that stole his breath. She was more than a bride; she was a vision of love, strength, and connection, embodying everything their bond represented.

His breath hitched as he drank in the sight. The mark pulsed faintly with their shared heartbeat, and he felt their connection thrumming like a live wire. His fingers reached out involuntarily, trembling as they traced the raised edges of his claim. The moment his skin touched the mark, she shivered, a soft gasp escaping her lips.

Tracing his own mark on her skin was intoxicating—he felt every nerve ending, every flutter of pulse beneath his touch. The scales were warm, almost fevered, seeming to shimmer brighter under his caress.

He leaned close, lips barely brushing her ear's shell, voice dropping to a husky whisper that weakened her knees. His free hand slid down to grip her possessively, fingers digging into silk.

"The things I'm going to do to you tonight will make the devil blush," he growled against her ear, hot breath sending shivers down her spine. "Now turn around and kiss me."

Sadie turned slowly, deliberately, movements as graceful as a dancer's. Her chestnut eyes, gold-flecked in afternoon light, bored into his with intensity that tightened his chest. A knowing smile played at her lips, equal parts innocent and wicked.

"Is that so, husband of mine?" she asked, her voice carrying a challenge that made his blood sing.

He grinned—predatory, possessive, completely captivated—and grabbed her, pulling her flush against his chest. Their bodies fit perfectly, two pieces of the same whole. When his lips crashed down on hers, the kiss was deep, claiming, full of months of restrained desire finally unleashed. She melted into him, hands fisting in his shirt fabric, matching his passion with fierce hunger.

The crowd erupted behind them—claps and cheers roaring from family and friends, mixed with playful whistles and good-natured catcalls. Their loved ones celebrated the passionate display, joy infectious as it filled the air around the newly bonded pair. Tonight would begin their forever journey.

# Chapter 31

Gaia sat at the kitchen table, sipping her raspberry tea. The warm, fragrant liquid offered comfort as she gazed out the bay windows, enchanted by the sight of a red fox playing with her two kits. Their playful antics made Gaia smile, a brief reminder of the joy of nurturing life. However, the smile was bittersweet. Parenting was undeniably both a blessing and a curse.

The blessing lay in the sheer miracle of bringing new life into the world, the indescribable joy of watching those tiny hands grow into something beautiful. But the curse was a heavy weight, one that came with the heart-wrenching experience of witnessing a child stumble and fall, filled with worry every time they stepped into the unknown, along with the sleepless nights spent waiting for their safe return.

Tartarus entered the kitchen as she let her thoughts drift down this familiar path. He wrapped his strong arms around her, pulled her close, and kissed her softly. In that moment, Gaia melted into his embrace, feeling as if the years of their marriage had melted away, leaving only the warmth of their love. Even after eternity together, he still had a way of taking her breath away.

"What has your attention, love?" he whispered gently in her ear, his voice soothing against her skin.

A soft sigh escaped her ruby red lips as memories washed over her. "I was just thinking about Damien when he was younger. He was so vibrant and full of life. But then I remember what she, the wrong one, did to him. She ripped his heart out. I can still see him holding his son's lifeless body in his arms for hours, and it feels as if that pain is etched into my heart."

Her eyes glistened as tears pooled, ready to spill. Tartarus's heart ached at the sight of her sorrow, and he could only recall that tragic day as vividly as she did. There were no words that could ever fully comfort a parent who had endured such loss. "My love," he said softly, "it was the hardest day of our lives. No parent should ever feel the loss of their child, not in body or spirit."

Gaia turned to face him fully, tears streaming down her face, underscoring the painful memories. "We lost our son that day. Not physically, of course, but mentally and emotionally… he was never the same."

With gentle hands, Tartarus wiped the tear stains from her cheeks, his touch as light as a feather yet filled with unwavering strength. "My beautiful flower, look at him now and how far he has come. He's had to work hard to reclaim his life, but he is doing it."

Her expression softened slightly, the corners of her mouth betraying a hint of a smile as she recalled a pivotal moment. "I remember when Bane came to me, his eyes sparkling with excitement. He told me about a blonde woman who had our son smiling again, bringing hope back into his heart. The hellhound was over the moon happy for him. She tore down the walls of his heart and showed him he was worthy of love once more."

A genuine smile brightened Gaia's face as she thought about Sadie, the girl who managed to breach the barriers Damien had built around himself. "Bane knew, even then, that Damien had found his soulmate. And it turned out he was right. Sadie breathed life back into our son. She gave him a purpose to fight for. Love truly is worth fighting for, isn't it?"

Tartarus leaned in and kissed Gaia's forehead, his heart swelling with gratitude. He understood the depth of her longing, the worry that had consumed them both.

"Sadie is his perfect match," he replied, smiling as he envisioned how Damien looked at her. "Her heart truly belongs to our son, which fills my heart with so much joy. And what's more, we're blessed to have a daughter now, a reflection of their love."

Gaia's eyes sparkled with a mix of pride and hope. "It's incredible how life can turn around, isn't it?" She sipped her tea, her thoughts drifting toward the future. "Who would have thought that light would emerge again from such darkness? Sadie has reminded Damien of the beauty in life, and now we are all living in that light together. She is also giving Damien the best gift he could ever receive. She doesn't know yet, but she is pregnant."

As they shared this moment, the warmth of their love wrapped around them like a comforting blanket. Together, they had faced countless storms, but now, as they stood on the brink of a new beginning, their hearts swelled with anticipation for the grandbaby on the way. They looked forward to the laughter and joy the little one would bring, eagerly sharing dreams of family gatherings, storytelling, and creating lasting memories that would weave their legacy even tighter.

***Two years later***

"Mama, catch me! Catch me!"

Luca's legs churned through the sand, his two-year-old stride barely keeping pace with his determination. Sadie watched him race ahead, salt wind whipping his dark hair across his forehead. Every morning brought this same miracle—waking up in a life she'd never dared dream possible.

The memory surfaced without invitation: discovering the pregnancy, terror freezing her tongue for weeks. Damien's loss of Ryder had carved something permanent from him, left him raw in ways that still ached when she touched his mind through her gift. They'd spoken of future children in whispers and maybes, content to weave themselves together first, to learn the rhythm of being husband and wife.

But bonds like theirs couldn't hide secrets for long.

——

She'd been kneeling beside Gaia in the herb garden, soil cool under her fingers as they transplanted rosemary for the kitchen terrarium. The sound of her name made her freeze mid-motion.

"Sadie?"

Something in Damien's voice—vulnerable, electric—made her stomach flip. She turned to find him standing in the garden archway, emotions warring across his features like storm clouds.

"What's wrong?" Her hands found his chest in three quick steps, searching his face. "Are you okay?"

"Everything is more than okay, lu me tesoro." His mouth claimed hers, that familiar fire sparking low in her belly. Then his palm settled over her stomach, and the world tilted. Those sparks became fireworks.

He knew. Of course, he knew.

"We're pregnant." The words tumbled out with her tears, relief, and terror tangled together.

"This I know, love." His thumb traced circles on her still-flat belly. "And I cannot wait for those little feet to fill our home with noise."

"I was going to tell you. I just needed to find the right moment."

"Sadie." His forehead touched hers, breath warm against her lips. "You pulled me from the grave I'd dug for myself. This baby exists because you taught me how to love again. Ryder will always live in my heart, but you showed me hearts can expand. This is just the beginning—I want to fill every room with laughter."

How had her gray, hollow existence transformed into this kaleidoscope of color and belonging? Sometimes the whiplash still left her breathless.

"I love you so much." She kissed him through salt tears, their bond igniting until—

"Ahem."

They broke apart to find Gaia grinning at them, dirt-stained hands on her hips.

"Now I can share my secret. I've known since your wedding night. Being all-powerful has its perks."

Gaia had become the mother Sadie never had, filling spaces she'd forgotten were empty. After the hugs and happy tears, Gaia clapped her hands together.

"Time to plan the baby shower. And before you protest, it's too early—this pregnancy won't last nine months. Immortal genetics, dear. Trust me." Her palm rubbed gentle circles on Sadie's stomach. "Six months, tops, and he'll be keeping us all awake."

"He?" Damien's voice caught on the word.

Gaia's smile could have powered the sun. "Yes, my son. You're having a boy."

—-

"Mama, run!"

Luca's shriek shattered her reverie as he sprinted past in the opposite direction, sand flying from his heels. From crawling to running overnight—and he hadn't slowed down since.

"Here I come!" She gave chase at half-speed, letting his stubby legs keep him ahead.

Luca—light—because that's exactly what he'd brought them. Luca Damien Ryder Nichols, carrying pieces of everyone who'd loved him before he even drew breath.

As if summoned by her thoughts, Damien materialized on the beach.

"Papa! Papa!"

Luca's speed doubled—an impossible feat—as he launched himself at his father. Damien caught him mid-air, tossed him skyward, then crushed him against his chest while Luca shrieked with delight.

Looking at them together was like seeing double—same dark hair, same olive skin, same piercing blue eyes. Both sets now focused entirely on her.

"Damien, you can't just appear out of thin air. What if someone saw you?"

"Down! Down!" Luca was already running in place against his father's chest.

"Run, Mama!" The words barely left his mouth before his feet hit sand, and he was off again, this time terrorizing a flock of seagulls.

"Listen, mate." Damien's arms encircled her waist, pulling her flush against him. "This is our private beach, and I checked with the guards first. But if you want to keep scolding me, I might just throw you over my shoulder and drag you back to my cave. I'm sure Grandmama would love some alone time with Luca while we work on giving him a sibling."

Love expanded in her chest until it hurt, spilling through their bond like wine from an overturned glass. His playful expression shifted, pupils dilating as the emotion hit him.

"I know, Sadie. It's the same for me. It always will be."

***The end***

## *A Future Glimpse Of...*

## *Her Hound*

### *Book 2 Of the Immortal Mark Saga*

Bane's first sensation was warmth, not the harsh heat of hellfire, but the gentle grip of hands that held him with reverence. As he opened his crimson eyes, still clouded with the newness of existence, he focused on the figure above him. Damien, the God of Monsters, looked down with a pride that seemed to illuminate the shadows of the underworld itself.

"Bane." The name flowed through his consciousness like an ancient incantation. Even as a fledgling creature, something stirred within him at the sound—a recognition of power and a destiny waiting to unfold.

The early days blurred together in a haze of rapid growth and insatiable hunger. Bane's small body pulsed with immortal energy, each heartbeat pushing him further from the vulnerable being he had once been. His limbs stretched longer, his midnight fur thickened, and those ember eyes began to blaze with an intelligence that startled even Damien.

But it was fire that changed everything.

Bane discovered it by accident—or perhaps it was fate, for nothing in the underworld truly happened by chance. Frustrated during a training session, snarling at his inability to meet Damien's expectations, he felt something ignite deep in his core. The sensation spread through his veins like molten gold, and suddenly he wasn't just a hellhound anymore. He was flame incarnate, his entire being transforming into a living inferno that danced and roared with his emotions.

"Extraordinary," Damien breathed, his voice filled with wonder—was that fear he saw in his eyes? "I created you to be powerful, but this... this is beyond my design."

Bane learned to control this transformation, shifting between flesh and fire at will. In his flame form, he could move like liquid lightning, his consciousness expanding to encompass every flicker and spark. He could sense the heat signatures of souls over vast distances, understanding the delicate balance between realms that Damien had spoken of so often.

Training intensified. Where once Damien had acted as a teacher and protector, he became something closer to an equal partner in their dark endeavors. Bane's abilities grew exponentially—he could track souls through dimensional barriers, burn away deception and lies with his hellfire, and stand shoulder to shoulder with ancient demons that had terrorized the underworld for eons.

Yet with this power came loneliness. Bane was unique, neither fully monster nor god, caught between realms in ways that left him aching with isolation. The other creatures of the underworld feared him, and rightly so. When he walked among them in his physical form, conversations ceased, and eyes dropped. As flame, they scattered like leaves before a storm.

Only with Damien did he feel truly understood. Their bond transcended creator and creation—they became partners in maintaining the cosmic balance, two sides of the same dark coin. Damien's strategic mind complemented Bane's raw power, creating a force that even the ancient powers of the underworld respected.

Then the war broke out.

When Hades grew reckless, allowing demons to flood the human realm unrestrained, Bane felt the disturbance in his very essence. The balance was fracturing, taking with it the careful order that had given his existence meaning. Standing beside Damien, surveying the chaos, Bane felt his flame form respond to his anger, disappointment, and fierce protective instincts.

"This ends now," he growled, his voice a low rumble echoing like the crackle of burning wood. The transformation came easier now, his physical form becoming a towering column of fire that dwarfed even Damien's impressive stature.

As they charged into battle, Bane discovered something new about himself. In combat, surrounded by enemies, his flame form became more than just fire—it became justice incarnate. Each foe felt not just his heat but also his judgment. Those who preyed on the innocent were consumed, while those who maintained honor in their darkness found his flames oddly gentle, clearing paths instead of devouring them.

The battles raged like storms, but Bane never tired. If anything, he grew stronger with each conflict, deepening his understanding of his own nature. He was not merely Damien's weapon or protector—he was a force of balance, born to stand at the crossroads between realms and ensure that neither chaos nor order could conquer completely.

When the last of Hades's reckless demons fell before his flames, Bane stood in the sudden silence, still filled with power yet finally at peace. He had discovered his purpose and identity. He was Bane, son of shadows, guardian of balance, and the living flame that would forever stand between the worlds.

Looking at Damien, who watched him with a mixture of pride and awe, Bane felt complete for the first time since his creation. He had become everything his creator envisioned and more—not just a monster born of darkness, but a being of light as well, burning bright enough to illuminate the path forward for all who would follow.

# Author Bio
## (Sitta Jayne)

Sitta Jayne weaves enchanting paranormal romance tales that find their way into readers' hearts and warm their souls. Her storytelling journey began six years ago, and she quickly found her voice in crafting supernatural love stories that blend the mystical with the romantic. After making her mark as an Amazon Vella author, Sitta took the next bold step in her writing career by publishing her first full-length novel through Native Publishing. Her transition from serial fiction to traditional publishing showcases her growth and dedication to her craft. When she's not creating magical worlds filled with supernatural romance, Sitta pours her passion into connecting with readers who share her love for paranormal tales. Her stories offer a safe haven for romance enthusiasts looking to escape into worlds where love transcends the ordinary.

# Author Bio
## (Everly Rose)

Everly's love of reading turned into a love of writing. One day, pen and paper in hand, a story unfolded with every stroke and she was hooked. Everly Rose is a rising author with the ability to lure her readers into the world's she creates. She is currently a co-author in the new release—Spellbound, book one of A Raven Series. And also Her Monster, book one in the Immortal Mark Saga. On top of that, there is a very loud demoness in her head, demanding her story be written. Stay tuned for that underworld narrative to unfold.

Books are proof that magic exists. Just open one and you'll see.

# Wanna Read More?

**Spellbound (The Raven Series #1)**
Written by Sitta Jayne & Everly Rose

https://a.co/d/bYv1iX9

# Meet the Authors

Sitta Jayne:
https://www.tiktok.com/@sittajayne2?_t=
ZT-8z31XNPbY0z&_r=1

Everly Rose:
https://facebook.com/61556361501530

Website:
https://www.sitta-jayne-and-everly-rose-authors.com/

# We would love a review

We really appreciate all your feedback and would love to hear from you.

Please leave us a review on Amazon or wherever you purchased this book from. We'd love to know what you thought of our first book in

## The Immortal Mark Saga

Thank you so much.

Sitta Jayne
&
Everly Rose